GUN COUNTRY

GUN COUNTRY

Wayne C. Lee

Chivers Press • Thorndike Press
Bath, England   Waterville, Maine USA

This Large Print edition is published by Chivers Press, England, and by Thorndike Press, USA.

Published in 2003 in the U.K. by arrangement with the author c/o Golden West Literary Agency.

Published in 2003 in the U.S. by arrangement with Golden West Literary Agency.

U.K. Hardcover ISBN 0–7540–8843–X (Chivers Large Print)
U.K. Softcover   ISBN 0–7540–8844–8 (Camden Large Print)
U.S. Softcover   ISBN 0–7862–4834–3 (Nightingale Series Edition)

The text of this Large Print edition is unabridged.
Other aspects of the book may vary from the original edition.

Set in 16 pt. New Times Roman.

Printed in Great Britain on acid-free paper.

British Library Cataloguing in Publication Data available

Library of Congress Cataloging-in-Publication Data

Lee, Wayne C.
    Gun country / Wayne C. Lee.
      p. cm.
    ISBN 0–7862–4834–3 (lg. print : sc : alk. paper)
    1. Inheritance and succession—Fiction. 2. Large type books.
  I. Title.
PS3523.E34457 G75 2003
813'.54—dc21
                                    2002073218

CHAPTER ONE

Brent Clark was within ten feet of the dead man before he saw him. He wouldn't have seen him then if it hadn't been for his horse. The horse snorted, nose toward the ground, then jerked up his head and shied off the trail.

Brent pulled back on the reins, halting the spooked horse. His eyes scanned the ground across the trail and saw the boots protruding from behind the rock. Nudging his horse to the nearest tree, he dismounted and tied the reins securely to a limb, then hurried back.

The man was sprawled behind the rock, a rifle just inches from his outstretched fingers where it had fallen from his hand. Blood was spread over his shirt from a wound in the back. It was that blood that had spooked Brent's horse.

Brent knelt beside the man, turning him just enough to see his face. He didn't know the man's name but he had seen him before. He worked for Jarron Dix on Dix's XD ranch. But what was he doing on Brent's ranch? His position suggested that he had been waiting here to ambush someone.

Brent frowned. He didn't like Jarron Dix and he didn't trust him at all. He even suspected Dix of being the man who had killed Aaron Clark, Brent's brother; or at least had

1

him killed, although he couldn't prove it. Had Dix sent this man to kill Brent? With Brent dead, there would be no one to keep Dix off the Clark ranch.

But who had killed this man? Brent looked for tracks around the body. There were none except his own. The man had been shot with a rifle, so the killer could have been some distance away.

A rumble of hoofbeats brought Brent's head up. A half-dozen riders were coming down the trail and when they saw him, they kicked their horses into a gallop. Brent recognized the huge frame of Jarron Dix himself at the head of the riders. Across his mind flashed the situation as Dix would see it—or pretend to see it. Dix's man was dead and Brent would be standing over him. He wheeled toward his horse tied to the tree limb some distance away. His rifle was still on his saddle. Even as he moved, he realized he could never reach his horse in time. Dix and his riders were too close. He turned to face them.

Dix slid his horse to a halt, his face set like an iron mask as he looked from the dead man to Brent. The men behind him waited grimly, their hands close to their guns. One man had his rifle out and lying across the horn of his saddle, the barrel almost directly in line with Brent.

'Well,' Dix rumbled, breaking the long silence, 'what do you have to say?'

'I was heading down to check my cattle at the lower end of the ranch when I came on this dead man. He's one of your men, isn't he?'

Dix nodded. 'I reckon you know that. How did you kill him?'

'I didn't,' Brent said, noting that another man had his gun out now and pointed it his way. 'What was he doing over here on my land, anyway?'

'Passing through,' Dix said. 'I sent him over to the south ranch this morning. When we got there, he hadn't shown up so we came back looking for him. I'm not too surprised to find him gunned down on your land.'

Brent knew he was up against a stacked deck. He didn't know who had killed this man and he doubted if Dix did, but that didn't matter. It was Brent that Dix wanted to get rid of, and he'd never get a better chance than this: to see that it was done—and blame it on justice.

'Want him beefed, boss?' the big man at Dix's left asked. He was even bigger than Dix. Brent knew him only as Nanz, the biggest man he had seen along Bitter Creek since he'd come here. Nanz stood six feet four and weighed at least two hundred and forty pounds.

'There are better ways than what you're thinking, Murdo,' Dix said. 'There are plenty of trees down along the creek.'

'We've got good ropes,' Murdo Nanz said

3

with a wolfish grin. 'Just say the word.'

'No point in waiting,' Dix said. 'Keep your gun on him, Jip.' He untied his rope and slowly fashioned a big slip knot in one end.

Brent watched him but his eyes darted to the other men, too. Three men held guns directly on him now, one with a rifle and two with six-guns. He wasn't even wearing his revolver this morning and his rifle might as well have been on its rack back at the house for all the good it could do him.

'Murdo, you can have the honor of tying his hands behind his back,' Dix said. 'Don't want him trying to claw the rope away from his neck. Takes too long for a man to die that way.'

The huge man swung down from saddle, his horse bracing himself to keep his balance as Nanz stepped to the ground. Brent waited, hoping Nanz would come between him and the men with the guns. He didn't have any illusions of being able to beat the big man with his fists but it would be better than docilely submitting to a rope around his neck.

Murdo Nanz, however, circled around to come up behind Brent, always keeping Brent exposed to those guns facing him. Raw fear was creeping into Brent now. He had never considered himself a coward but he was no fool, either. He was facing death, eye to eye. He could swear that he hadn't killed Dix's man, but that wouldn't change the outcome.

Brent heard the heavy footsteps behind him. Then Nanz grabbed his hands and jerked them together behind his back. Brent felt the rope bite into his wrists as Nanz yanked it tight.

'Mike was my buddy,' Nanz said in Brent's ear. 'I'm going to enjoy seeing you dance on air.'

'I didn't kill him,' Brent couldn't help saying, even though he knew it was wasted breath.

'Of course not,' Nanz said sarcastically. 'It was a rifle. We're not going to hang you, either. It'll be the rope.' He gave Brent a shove. 'Get to your horse.'

Brent stumbled toward his horse. Before he reached it, another of Dix's men moved past him and jerked the rifle from the saddle boot.

'There's a big cottonwood down by the creek,' Dix said, pointing. 'We'll go down there.'

Nanz grabbed Brent and half lifted him into the saddle. He then untied the reins of the horse and led Brent back to his own horse. The party of seven riders left the trail and moved down the slope to the river bottom. Nanz led Brent's horse under the cottonwood tree and looked up, searching for a strong limb. Finding it, he stopped the horse.

Dix rode up beside Brent, flipping the end of the rope over the big limb. Then he dropped the noose over Brent's head, sliding the knot down against his neck.

Brent was numb now. It was as if he were detached from the scene, looking down on it with only a mild interest. He noted the satisfaction in Jarron Dix's pale blue eyes and he thought foolishly how alike Dix and his big gunman were. Dix was six feet three and weighed two hundred and twenty pounds with light, almost blond, hair. Murdo Nanz, even bigger, had faded brown hair and unemotional slate-colored eyes that reminded Brent of a dead snake.

'Anything to say before you sprout wings?' Dix asked.

'What good would it do? I didn't kill that man.'

Dix nodded grimly. 'I didn't expect you'd admit it. You're as bullheaded as your brother.'

'At least you *shot* him instead of hanging him,' Brent said.

'I didn't—' Dix began, then snorted, 'What difference does it make what you believe? Let's get it over with, Murdo.'

Murdo Nanz moved back to give the horse a slap on the rump. But he stopped with his hand raised as a rifle shot ripped through the branches of the tree.

'Just everybody sit still!' someone shouted from a small grove of willows less than thirty yards from the cottonwood.

Brent snapped his head around along with the others. There was no one in sight, but the rifle barrel was very visible.

After a moment of stunned immobility, one of Dix's men swung his gun toward the willows. The rifle barked again, the man yelled and dropped his gun, grabbing his arm from which blood began to spurt.

'I said for everybody to sit tight,' the voice repeated calmly. 'Is there anyone else who wants to argue the point?'

When no one said anything, the rifle moved just slightly to center on Murdo Nanz. 'Back off, Nanz.'

Nanz pulled his horse back beside Dix. Then a man stepped out of the willows, his rifle cocked and moving slowly to give every man the impression it was pointed directly at him. He was an average-sized man but small in comparison with Dix and Nanz. His hair that had once been brown, now was streaked with gray.

Brent couldn't believe the miracle that was happening. He had been so sure he was going to die that he almost felt dead. He certainly wouldn't have expected help from Frank Zarada even if he had known he was in those willows. Zarada had never struck Brent as a violent man. And it took a man with a streak of violence in him to shoot another man in the arm as calmly as Zarada had winged Dix's man.

'Now all of you, back away your horses about ten yards,' Zarada said. 'I won't just wing the next one. I don't know how you figure you have a right to hang a man on his own tree.'

'He killed one of my men,' Dix growled, as he backed away his horse along with the rest.

'What jury says so?' Zarada asked. 'You ain't the whole law here, Dix.'

'Mike was my man and we found Brent Clark leaning over him to make sure he was dead.' Dix said. 'Who are you to say he goes free?'

'I don't say he goes free; just that he gets a fair trial. A lynching sure don't qualify. Now unbuckle your gun belts one by one, starting with you Dix.'

Dix scowled at Zarada. 'You're going to be sorry you butted in,' he growled.

'I'm going to butt in with this rifle if you don't drop your gun,' Zarada said calmly. 'That goes for rifles, too.'

Dix swore but he dropped his rifle, and then let his gun belt fall on top of it. The man next to him did the same. When all the revolvers and rifles were on the ground, Zarada motioned with his rifle barrel.

'Back those horses off about twenty yards. Then dismount and take off the saddles.'

'Going to steal our horses, too?' Dix grumbled.

'Just making sure you don't get in too big a hurry to follow me.'

When the men were on the ground twenty

8

yards from their guns, their horses unsaddled, Zarada motioned for Brent to follow him. Touching spurs to his horse, Zarada galloped down the valley. With his hands still tied behind his back Brent was hard pressed to keep pace.

He turned his head to see four of Dix's men slapping saddles back on their horses, while the other two were running for their guns.

All Brent had gained was a reprieve. Dix and his men were not about to give up. There were six of them and only two of him and Zarada. He could still feel that rope around his neck.

CHAPTER TWO

Brent's horse carried him around a bend and out of sight of Dix's men before they could reach their guns. But it would be no more than a few minutes until they were saddled-up and armed again, ready to take up the pursuit. He wondered if Zarada had a plan to elude Dix's men.

Then he realized with a shock that Zarada was heading directly for his own house, making no effort to hide a thing. Zarada reined up in front of the house and Brent's horse pulled up, too.

'Forgot about your hands being tied,'

9

Zarada said. 'That must have been a rough ride.'

'Better than riding without a horse like Dix planned,' Brent said. 'We're not stopping here, are we?'

Zarada shrugged and got the ropes off Brent's wrists, and Brent dismounted. Zarada led the horses toward the barn.

'Won't they come here looking for us?' Brent demanded.

'Not till they get the sheriff. Dix knows he overstepped himself. He'll bring the law next time.'

'Rudy Grubb is Dix's man, isn't he?' Brent argued.

'Body and soul,' Zarada nodded as he led the way to the house. 'But it'll take a while for Dix to find Rudy. Before they get here, I've got a proposition for you. So come on in where we can talk.'

Reluctantly, Brent followed Zarada inside. He wanted to get away from here now but Zarada was determined to tell him something he considered important and Brent did owe Zarada some time, if nothing else for saving his live.

Just before going inside, Brent looked back up the valley. There was no sign of Dix's men but he knew they wouldn't quit just because Zarada had thwarted them momentarily.

'Make it fast,' Brent said as he stepped inside. 'I don't like having my neck stretched.'

Zarada tossed his hat on a chair and sprawled out in a big arm chair in front of the fireplace he had built in one end of his living room. Brent's whole house wasn't much bigger than Zarada's living room.

'There are some things you don't know about Jarron Dix that I do,' Zarada said. 'One's that he wants the Pool ranch so bad he can taste it, but he knows better than to twist my tail to get it.'

Brent frowned and dropped into a chair facing Zarada. 'Are you going to give it to him?'

'Let me tell you the whole story. All you probably know is that your brother was leasing the Pool ranch from the estate and I'm the administrator of the estate.'

Brent nodded. 'That's about it except that Dix swore I had no claim to the lease after Aaron was killed. Your lawyer proved that I inherited the lease from Aaron.'

Zarada nodded. 'Henry Pool was my best friend. We both worked for John Eliff out along the South Platte. Then Henry got married and his wife brought along a tidy little fortune. Henry bought out twenty homesteaders who had settled along Bitter Creek, taking up the creek in forty- and eighty-acre chunks for over twelve miles. The ranchers and Indians just wouldn't let them stay here, though. Three or four were killed. The rest jumped at the chance to sell out to

Henry.'

'What's that got to do with Jarron Dix?' Brent asked impatiently.

Zarada held up his hand. 'I'm coming to that.'

Brent wished he would hurry. His mind was only half on what Zarada was saying. The rest was listening for the approach of horses.

'Henry Pool was shot from ambush and a day later his young wife and year-and-a-half-old daughter were run off a high bluff on the way to town to the funeral. Henry had a will and he had named me as administrator of his estate. He left everything to his wife, Lela, or if she was dead, to his daughter, Virginia, to be given to her on her eighteenth birthday.'

'What was to happen to it if she was dead?'

'Then Henry's cousin, Jarron Dix, was to get it.'

Brent was jolted by the news that Jarron Dix was Henry Pool's cousin. 'Why didn't Dix get the ranch then?'

'Because nobody could give me positive proof that the daughter, Virginia, was dead. Some neighbors had seen Lela and Virginia start to town and they followed about a half hour later. They found the wreck with Lela dead but the little girl was missing. Her bonnet and one shoe were in the wrecked wagon but they couldn't find the girl. Everybody's sure she crawled off somewhere and died. But I've held out for proof of her death before turning

12

over the Pool ranch to Dix.' Zarada leaned forward. 'Now I've a proposition that might keep the Pool ranch lease for you.'

'Want me to prove this girl is still alive?'

'More than that,' Zarada said. 'I want you to bring her here. Virgie's eighteenth birthday, if she's still alive, is a week from today. The estate will be settled that day. If Virgie Pool isn't in Greeley to claim her inheritance, then Jarron Dix gets Pool ranch. You know where that puts you.'

Brent glanced nervously out the window. 'If I stick around here, I'll be so dead it won't make any difference.'

'You're safer with me than by yourself,' Zarada said. 'Dix wants me to stay alive till I have to turn Pool over to him. Otherwise, he'll face a long legal battle which he doesn't want. If you bring Virgie in for the estate settlement, it will keep Pool out of Dix's hands. And Virgie will surely let you keep the lease.'

'That sounds good,' Brent admitted. 'But where will I find Virgie Pool? If she is alive, why hasn't she shown up before?'

'I think she's in Gunsight Canyon,' Zarada said, leaning forward, the light from the window glinting off his graying hair. 'A man named Kurtzman has a sheep ranch in the canyon, and he says he has a crazy son. He put a guard at the canyon mouth and won't let anyone in because he's afraid they'll take his boy away and put him in an asylum.'

'You think the Pool girl is there?'

'I'm sure of it. Kurtzman has a wife, three sons and a daughter. It's that daughter I'm interested in. Joel Kurtzman came to see me and hinted that he and I could share Pool if we worked it right.'

'What'd he mean by that?' Brent asked, interested in spite of his uneasiness.

'I think his daughter is really Virgie Pool and he figures he can make Virgie do anything he says. He can't get the Pool ranch legally, though, without help, and he's willing to share Pool if I'll cooperate with him.'

'That might be better than letting Dix have it.'

'Maybe. But I don't trust Kurtzman as far as I can throw a bull by the tail. I went up to take a look for myself. Had to climb over the ridge into the back side of the canyon, past the tall rock that gives the canyon the name of Gunsight. I hid out until I saw all the family. There is a girl there and she's about eighteen. Even more important, she's the very image of Lela Pool. I'm positive she's Virgie.'

'And you want me to bring her out?'

Zarada nodded. 'It won't be easy. Anyway, you can't stay here with Dix determined to hang you. If you run, you'll lose everything you have in Pool. But if you can get Virgie Pool to that estate settlement in Greeley, you'll likely get a long lease on Pool for your effort. It's your choice.'

14

'Dix will still get me hanged for murder.'

'If you can prove that Virgie Pool is alive, it'll give me some facts that I think will show Dix's brand from the under side.'

'What can I expect up there in Gunsight Canyon?' Brent asked.

'That's gun country,' Zarada said. 'Joel Kurtzman's determined to keep all strangers out of the canyon. He's done a good job of it, too. He's been there about three years and nobody could even prove there was a girl up there until I went up and got a good look. He says his crazy boy won't hurt anybody, but he won't let him out of the canyon.'

'What will he do to a stranger?'

'No worse than Joel himself will do, that's sure. The boy does have a big dog—a mixed breed, mostly mastiff, that looks vicious. I saw him and I gave him plenty of room. You'll be wise to do the same. Now if Dix finds out about the girl, he'll try to kill her. He can't legally own Pool while she's alive. And Kurtzman has every intention of owning Pool himself so he'll kill anyone who tries to get Virgie out of there. You can bet on that. He's his own law up there. Nothing short of an army could root him out. So, you'll have to steal her.'

'Will she come with me?'

'I doubt if she'll come willingly. She was only a year-and-a-half old when the accident happened. She probably can't remember anything that happened before. She likely thinks she's a Kurtzman herself.'

'And I'll get killed while I'm trying to get her away,' Brent said sarcastically.

Zarada nodded. 'You take that chance. And you've got only a week to get her to Greeley for the settlement of the estate.'

Brent weighed the chances in his mind. He could just ride out of the country. He'd lose what he had in Pool, but he'd be alive. On the other hand, if he went into Gunsight Canyon, he'd run a big chance of never coming out. However, if he did go, he might keep Dix from getting Pool and save his own interest in the ranch.

He hadn't yet reached a decision when he heard the faint thunder of galloping horses.

'That'll be Dix and he'll have the sheriff with him,' Zarada said calmly. 'You'll have to make up your mind.'

Brent knew he had waited too long already. Those riders were coming fast. He could never get to the barn and get his horse before they caught him.

CHAPTER THREE

'I've listened to you jabber too long,' Brent said angrily, glancing out the window. He saw six or seven horses galloping hard toward the house.

16

Zarada seemed undisturbed. 'You had to know these things. I leased Pool to your brother in good faith and I made sure you got the lease when he was killed. I want you to keep it.'

Brent wheeled on Zarada. 'Looks more like you want to get me killed. You know what Dix'll do when he gets me.'

Zarada nodded. 'If he gets you. Seeing a deer and killing him are two different things.'

'My horse is in the barn. Dix and his outfit will get to the barn before I can.'

'That isn't the only horse in the world,' Zarada said. 'How about going after Virgie?'

Brent stared at Zarada in exasperation. 'Dix is here to hang me, and all you can think about is getting that girl out of the canyon!'

'That's right. If you get her out, you'll keep Dix from getting Pool. And, you might even pin some other crimes on him—such as your brother's murder.'

'How will finding Virgie Pool do that?'

'You never know how much water is going to leak out till you puncture the barrel.' Zarada got up and headed for the kitchen with Brent at his heels. 'You'll need some grub. Kurtzman ain't going to feed you up there in his canyon. You'll need a revolver, a rifle, and some ammunition, too.'

The thunder of hoofbeats stopped suddenly in the front yard. Brent recognized Dix's bass voice as he yelled.

'Frank, you got that murderer in there?'

'There's no murderer in here,' Zarada yelled back, motioning to Brent to fill the sack he was holding out.

Brent gabbed some bread, some fried ham, a slab of bacon, coffee, a box of matches and a couple of boxes of ammunition while Zarada went back to the living room to the window looking out into the yard.

'Better trot him on out if he's in there,' a new voice called.

'I said there was no murderer in here, Grubb,' Zarada yelled back. 'Now if you're friendly, you can come in for some coffee, but if you're bent on trouble, just ride on out. I've got my rifle and I ain't afraid to use it.'

'I'm the law,' Grubb shouted back. 'Jarron says you took a prisoner away from him this morning.'

'Since when was he authorized to take a prisoner?'

There was a silence in the yard as Brent finished putting the food and ammunition into the sack, and then picked up the gun, belt and rifle that Zarada had laid out. He thought how ridiculous it was to be preparing so carefully for a trip into the mountains when a posse was in the front yard demanding his hide. Yet Zarada had seemed totally confident and Brent had absorbed some of that confidence.

'Hey,' a muffled voice shouted. 'Here's the horse he was riding. He's around here somewhere.'

Brent stepped into the partition doorway. 'Now they've got my horse. How do I get away?'

Zarada spoke without turning his attention from the window. 'Slip out my bedroom window. There's that chokecherry thicket just a few feet from the window. It runs into a ravine. Follow that ravine down about a quarter of a mile. You'll find my little white pony there, in the corner of the pasture. She's always there this time of day. Gentle as a lamb. You'll have to ride bareback but you can keep to the ravine. You should get away easy enough. When you get as close to Gunsight Canyon as the horse can take you, turn her loose. She'll come home. You'll have to go in by Gunsight Rock. It's the only way you can make it.'

'What about Dix and Grubb when they find you've let me get away?'

'Dix won't bother me—not until after he gets Pool. Better start moving. They're getting restless.'

Brent turned into the bedroom Zarada had indicated. He heard the yelling in the front yard and knew they were going to break into the house at any moment to search for him. Buckling on the gun belt and grabbing the sack of grub and rifle, he crossed to the window which was already up. He heard the pounding on the door behind him as he swung a leg over

19

the window sill.

Dropping to the ground, he glanced both ways. Nobody was in sight but the racket at the front of the house was increasing. He had waited too long. Dix and Grubb were going to break into the house any second now. When they discovered he was gone, they'd begin a search. Once they found him, he'd be a dead man.

He ran toward the chokecherry thicket, bending low. The farther from the house he got, the less protection he had from the eyes of those in the front yard. Reaching the thicket, he dived inside. Catching his breath, he moved through the thicket to the edge of the ravine. There he suddenly stopped, sinking as low into the bushes as he could.

Someone was coming. Peering through the leaves of the chokecherries, he made out a man moving quietly up the ravine toward the back of the house. Sheriff Rudy Grubb had his attention focused on the house. Brent was surprised that the sheriff hadn't seen him crawl out the window. He guess Grubb hadn't been close enough to see the house then.

Grubb hesitated behind the chokecherries bushes, apparently trying to decide the best way to approach the house. Or, maybe he was just going to wait here to make sure Brent didn't escape out the back while Dix went in the front way.

Brent practically held his breath, something

close to panic was building in him. Every second he lost here meant that much less chance he had of getting away. He didn't fool himself into thinking he could survive against Dix and the sheriff and Dix's five men. His only chance lay in running before they could find him. But he couldn't move now.

Grubb stared at the chokecherry bushes and Brent was sure he would see him there. But after a minute, Grubb moved on up the ravine toward the house. Brent could hear yelling at the house and he was sure that Dix had finally gotten inside. It was that commotion that had drawn Grubb up nearer the house.

As soon as the sheriff was past the bushes, Brent slipped into the ravine and headed away from the house, running in a crouch. He came to a fence across the ravine and crawled through the wire. He heard a horse snort before he saw the white pony. She was in the corner of the pasture as Zarada had said she would be and she was snorting her displeasure at being interrupted in her morning nap.

Brent glanced back toward the house but it was out of sight. Climbing out of the ravine, he walked slowly toward the horse, talking soothingly to it. Zarada had said she was gentle and the little horse proved him right. She cocked her ears forward and eyed him suspiciously but she didn't back away more than a couple of steps.

Clutching the little horse by the mane with

the hand that held the rifle, he swung onto her back, holding the sack of grub in his other hand. He had no saddle or bridle but he discovered that she guided easily by pressure from his knees.

He turned the pony into the ravine that paralleled the pasture fence and headed toward the mountains. He remembered the pasture, and knew there was a gate not far from this ravine at the far side of it. He'd have to leave the ravine there and go through the gate. Beyond that, he'd try to keep out of sight while he made his way to the mountains.

He found the gate, slid off the pony's back and opened it, then led the pony through. The pony wasn't much for speed, but she seemed mighty fast compared to being afoot.

Mounting again, he pointed the little white horse toward the mountains and put her to a lope. She was too old to move very fast or run very long, so he only let her run for a short distance. He wished he had his big rangy bay. Then he'd be able to outrun his pursuers if they saw him, but he could never outrun them on this pony.

As he neared the mountains, he aimed the pony toward the smaller of two canyons that led into the high country. He knew that Dix and Grubb would look for him and if they decided he was heading for the hills, they'd expect him to take the big canyon. Gunsight Canyon opened into the big canyon, but

Zarada had said that Kurtzman kept a guard at the mouth of Gunsight Canyon. The only other way in was by way of Gunsight Rock at the upper end of the canyon. This smaller canyon that ended in the high country would take Brent as close to Gunsight Rock as a horse could go.

However, before he reached the mountains, he saw dust back on the plains to the east and guessed that Dix, Grubb and the XD men were after him. Brent recognized his danger. He was already well up off the plains, heading for the canyon, but he knew that Zarada's little white pony would be visible for miles on this bare slope.

Kicking the pony in the ribs, Brent pushed upward toward the canyon. There was no place here he could hide. If they saw him, his only chance would be to get into the hills far enough so that he could find a place to disappear before they reached the canyon.

Looking back, he saw the dust trail continuing to bend his way. They had spotted him, and soon would have him trapped in this dead-end canyon. It could be a dead end for him, too. He had planned to climb up the canyon wall to Gunsight Rock and down into Gunsight Canyon. Without pursuit, that shouldn't be so hard, but with Dix and Grubb so close on his trail, Brent knew it would be next to impossible.

Urging the little white pony to its best

effort, he headed directly into the canyon. No faking now would throw his pursuers off the trail. The pony labored up the steep slope to the mouth of the canyon. There were no trees on the slope, only sage and coarse grass struggled to cover the dirt that washed out of the canyon in the heaviest rains. Brent had never felt so exposed to the world as he did now, pushing the white pony over the bare expanse, a couple of hundred feet above the level of the plains below.

Twisting to look back, Brent saw the dust plume moving toward him with frightening speed. Dix's men had good horses and they were still on comparatively level ground. At this rate, Brent wouldn't be much further than just entering the mouth of the canyon when Dix's men reached the foot of the slope.

The men behind were close enough for Brent to distinguish the individuals by the time the little pony had scrambled up to the lip of the slope where the ground slanted only gradually upward into the canyon. Brent urged the horse into a steady trot, and it was obvious that she was too tired to go faster.

Once inside the mouth of the canyon, he found a few trees again. Here there were stretches of bare rock in the bottom of the canyon where rushing water scoured away the dirt after each hard rain. That dirt had piled up at the mouth of the canyon, forming the steep slope up which he had come.

Brent knew he had only a short time to find some way to elude his pursuers. With their long legged horses, they would come up that slope much faster than he had. His eyes searched the walls on either side of the canyon. They looked impossible to climb but he knew they were not. Frank Zarada had climbed that wall to get into Gunsight Canyon, and Zarada was neither a young man nor a particularly agile one. Finding where he had ascended would be the problem for Brent. If only he could locate it immediately, he would try to climb out of reach of Dix's men before they arrived. But he saw no place where a man could climb to safety in the few minutes he had.

Water had rushed down from the tops of the canyon on either side, cutting side canyons that were narrow and had almost perpendicular sides. In some of them, there was enough dirt to sprout trees and brush.

Brent kept looking back although he knew his pursuers couldn't be showing up yet, even with their good horses.

Then his attention was caught by a strip of washed clean rock right at the mouth of a little side canyon. This pocket was deeper than most, reaching back a hundred yards into the main wall. Trees choked the little canyon only a short distance from the mouth. Brent stopped the pony and examined the side pocket with his eyes. He rode on ten yards to a narrow patch of dirt that had formed a ridge across the bare rock. Riding across this, he made sure his horse's prints would be easily seen. He then kneed the pony sharply to his right, along the rock, finding a littered area where he could turn his horse back to the smooth rock in front of the side pocket.

The little pony crossed this debris leaving such slight tracks that they would be visible only upon the closest examination. Brent then turned the little pony into the side pocket. At the edge of the brush and trees, he dismounted and found a place where he was able to worm into the thicket and pull the unwilling pony after him. Far enough back inside the grove to be out of sight of the main canyon, he stopped.

He had no fear that his weary pony would leave the shelter they had found, but he would have to make sure she didn't whinny when she caught the scent of the other horses. With his rifle ready to swing into use, he stood beside the pony's head and waited.

The little horse raised her head suddenly. Brent pressed a hand over her nose to stifle a whinny. He hadn't heard the approaching horses yet but the pony had. A minute later, he heard the click of horses' hoofs on the rock in the main canyon.

Waiting, one hand still on the horse's nose, the other gripping his rifle, Brent watched the mouth of the little side canyon through the trees. He saw the riders file past. Then one of them shouted back to the others that the tracks led on.

Brent held his breath. Would they see that no tracks went on up the canyon? Would they find the tracks where the pony had come back across that debris?

The sounds out in the canyon faded as the riders went on. But the canyon was not a long one and ended in a solid rock wall. When the men came back, they'd search more carefully. They'd see where he had backtracked into this side canyon. He had, at best, again only a short reprieve.

Moving out to the mouth of the little pocket, he glanced up the canyon. The horses and riders were still in view, moving slowly as though they had already discovered that their prey had not gone this way.

Running back, Brent reached a quick decision. He led the white pony out to the mouth of the pocket. The riders were not in sight now. Pointing the pony toward the mouth of the canyon and the plain beyond, he gave her a slap on the hip and watched her trot wearily toward the plains.

Afoot now with only a six-gun, rifle, and a sack filled with food and ammunition, he headed back into the pocket. If there was no way out of this pocket up the cliff, he'd find a spot to make his stand. He'd have no other choice. He had no illusion that Dix's men would give up without searching every side pocket in this canyon.

CHAPTER FOUR

Before reaching the trees, Brent searched the canyon walls above him. Trees grew here and there in cracks in the rock but the wall didn't look too steep to climb. According to his memory of this area, and he'd only been up here once, he must be almost behind Gunsight Canyon now. If he could get to the top of this canyon wall, he should be able to locate Gunsight Rock.

Getting away from Dix's men was his first job. Beating his way through the brush, he broke out of the trees to find himself in a narrow trough down which water poured when it rained. He was able to scramble up this trough. In only a minute, he was above the level of the treetops in the pocket. A short distance above, he hit a ledge, and it appeared to him that there had been some kind of travel along it, probably some animal trail. If an animal could go along here, he could, too. And, if animals used it, it must lead somewhere. Anywhere was better than staying here where Dix's men could find him.

The ledge led upward toward the high peaks along the divide. Brent kept his eyes on the canyon below because he now was heading in the same direction Dix's men had gone. Then the ledge faded out, but there was a trough filled with rubble leading up to what appeared to be another ledge. Without hesitation, Brent started scrambling up this trough. He reached the next ledge and found it angled back the way he had come but sharply upward. Fifty yards ahead, a tree had forced its roots into a crack in the rock, splitting the rock and collecting soil in the split until it had grown twenty feet tall.

He had barely reached the tree and stopped to catch his breath when he caught a glimpse of Dix's men coming back down the canyon. They were moving very slowly, checking for tracks and sending one rider into every side pocket. Brent stepped behind the tree where he hoped he wouldn't be noticed from below.

What would happen when Dix's men found the pocket where he'd gone in and hadn't come out? Would they start up the wall as he had done? He fingered his rifle. He didn't want to shoot anybody but if they came after him, he intended to make them pay dearly for his death.

The searchers reined up at the side pocket where Brent had hidden himself and the white pony. But instead of a man coming into the pocket to search, one rider waved frantically and pointed to the ground. Brent realized the man was seeing the tracks the little white pony had made as she left the pocket and headed back for home.

With a surge, the riders moved ahead, going

at a lope now, following the easy trail left by the pony. Brent waited only until they went around a slight bend in the canyon before moving on up the ledge. When they caught sight of the pony, they'd see that she had no rider and they might turn back. He had to be out of sight before they returned.

The ledge was steep and at times dangerously narrow, but he kept scrambling ahead, careful not to drop his rifle or sack of provisions. The air was thin, so he had to stop and rest often, but the threat of the return of Dix's men kept him pushing ahead. At last, after what seemed hours to him, Brent reached the crest of the ridge that separated the dead-end canyon from the bigger canyon beyond. The big canyon ran at a different angle from the one he had come into. As deep as he was in the mountains now, that other canyon might be several miles to the north of him. Between this ridge and that big canyon were several side canyons, some of them of major proportions themselves. Gunsight Canyon was one of these, walled in on three sides and with a mouth so narrow that it could be guarded by one man. That was likely the reason Joel Kurtzman had chosen it for his sheep ranch.

Sprawling out on the first level spot he had seen in two hours, Brent tried to catch his breath and revive his aching muscles. The sun was hot up here in the thin atmosphere but the air itself was chilly.

When he lifted his head and looked around, he spotted Gunsight Rock almost immediately. It was only a quarter of a mile to the west, backed up against the ridge. It appeared from here to be no more than ten feet higher than the ridge itself, but Brent had heard that from the bottom of Gunsight Canyon, it seemed to stick up at the boxed end of the canyon like a finger pointing to the sky. To a hunter, it might appear very much like the sight on the end of a rifle barrel.

Getting to his feet, Brent moved along the ridge to the spire, this unmistakable landmark of Gunsight Canyon. He stopped beside it and looked down into the valley. Brent doubted the valley below, boxed in on both sides by steep walls, could be climbed even by a mountain goat. Down at the mouth of the canyon, Brent could see the gap that opened out into the main canyon. It was a good three miles away and, from this distance, the gap didn't look wide enough to drive a wagon through. But while he knew it was at least fifty yards wide, Brent reminded himself that one man probably controlled every movement in that opening from a hiding place in the rocks on either side.

Knowing he had to get down into that canyon in a hurry to get out of view of any straying eyes in the valley below, Brent began searching for a trail down the steep slope. This descent wasn't going to be nearly as hard as the climb up the other side. Kurtzman obviously depended on the steep wall on the opposite side of the ridge to keep strangers out of the canyon from this end. No one was going to come into the canyon from either side, that was sure.

A third of the way down the steep slope, Brent came across a trail that evidently led up to Gunsight Rock from the canyon below. He began following it cautiously, and noted fresh tracks in the trail which showed that it had been used recently.

Far below, perhaps halfway down the length of the canyon, Brent could see the buildings of Kurtzman's ranch. A stream, fed by melting snow and probably springs, flowed past the buildings. Sheep corrals were in front of a long, low shed. The house was some distance from the sheep sheds. Sheep were in two separate flocks, grazing between Brent and the buildings, guarded by dogs. He saw no sign of anybody anywhere.

As he neared the bottom of the slope, he saw cow tracks on the trail and stopped, frowning. Kurtzman was a sheepman; he wouldn't have cattle. Brent turned to search the pockets near him and saw two big steers grazing on the rich grass. Even at this distance, he could read the brands. One was XD, Jarron Dix's brand, and the other was Pool, his own brand. The Pool brand was a big circle with four bars radiating out from the circle. Some might call it the sun. Since it had belonged to Henry Pool, Brent and his brother had kept it as the official Pool brand. The Kurtzmans evidently liked some beef to give variety to their mutton diet. If what Brent had heard about Joel Kurtzman was true, it wouldn't bother his conscience to get his beef the easy way instead of raising it.

Suddenly Brent's attention was caught by a stone rolling down the slope ahead of him. Someone or something was on the trail. Brent glided off the trail into some shrubs and sank down out of sight. He saw a boy coming up the trail preceded by a huge dog. That would be Joel Kurtzman's crazy son and his vicious dog that Zarada had warned Brent about. The boy carried a rifle like he knew how to use it.

Brent could keep out of sight of the boy, but that dog would surely pick up his scent. The dog was much bigger than a shepherd, with heavy shoulders and a huge, square-nosed head. His massive legs were set far apart. However mixed up his ancestry might be, it was evident that the mastiff blood had dominated. Brent had seen pictures of mastiffs but he had never seen one in the flesh and, under the present circumstances, the sight was not one that brought joy to his heart. The dog looked like he could easily tear a man apart and enjoy every second of it.

Brent wished his rifle was around where he

could lever a shell into the chamber if he needed it. But it wasn't, and any move he made would certainly bring instant detection.

Brent held his breath as the boy and dog came closer. He was surprised at the size of Tolly. From what Zarada had said, he had expected a shrunken, undersized youngster. Tolly was almost grown, only three or four inches shorter than Brent himself, and probably weighed almost as much. His face, however, was young and had the happy, rather blank look of one who had few worries and spent very little time fretting about them.

Brent's attention, however, centered on the dog. The big animas was sniffing along the trail as if searching for something on which to vent some inner fury. Brent knew he'd have to move swiftly to protect himself if the dog caught his scent. Then, just a few feet before he reached Brent's level, the dog stopped and lifted his ugly muzzle, sniffed a time or two, then wheeled off the trail and charged toward the meadow where the two big steers were grazing.

The boy ran after him, calling sharply at the dog. When the dog didn't heed the call, the boy swore violently and yelled louder.

'Tolliver, you come back here. If you chew up one of those steers, Pa will kill you for sure.'

The dog reached the meadow and the two steers, sensing their danger, turned to face the

34

dog, and their heads lowered with horns swinging menacingly. The boy was running like a deer, almost keeping up with the dog which was suddenly having second thoughts about the fun he'd have working over the two steers who obviously wanted no part of the game. The dog suddenly stopped and turned back to the boy as if he had just heard Tolly's call. The mastiff evidently had hunting blood in him.

Brent waited, wondering if the boy could call the dog off a man if he went for him like he had the steers. Brent knew that he wouldn't look half as menacing to that dog as those two steers had.

The boy and dog headed on toward Gunsight Rock but they angled toward the trail from the meadow, bypassing Brent's hiding place by several yards. Brent waited until they had reached the trail fifty yards above him and had moved out of earshot; then he slipped quietly out of the shrubs and moved on down the trail.

Before reaching the valley floor, he left the trail and moved along the east side of the canyon. The perpendicular wall stretched up above him and he could see that he had been right in his first estimate, that no one could climb into the valley over that wall. The lower part of the wall scaled off into a shale slope. Just below the shale a belt of aspens grew, covering much of the rough shale from the sight of those in the bottom of the valley.

Brent made his way through the aspens. They afforded him a view of the canyon floor while hiding his movements. He reached the middle of the canyon opposite the buidings of Kurtzman's ranch and stopped, watching the ranch for several minutes. He saw a woman come out of the house, shade her eyes against the sun and peer up the canyon in the direction that the boy and his dog had gone. There were two flocks of sheep up the canyon and only a half-dozen dogs seemed to be guarding them. Brent knew there was little need to watch them. There was no way the sheep could get out of the canyon except to go past the house and out through the mouth of the canyon.

No men appeared at the house and Brent moved on toward the gateway into the main canyon. He stopped a couple of hundred yards from the canyon's mouth and watched the entrance. It took him only a minute to spot the guard, hidden from the entrance by a nest of boulders. He was sitting there half asleep, a rifle across his knees. But no one could slip into the canyon without alarming him for the canyon mouth was hard rock, scoured clean by the small stream running through it. Joel Kurtzman had a secure hideout that would do credit to an outlaw's dream.

Brent went back the way he came, staying among the aspens, out of sight of the canyon floor. Up along the shale slopes, he spotted several holes with platforms of rock and dust in front of them, the tailings from the mines reaching down into the edge of the trees. None of the mines showed any signs of having been worked recently. Apparently this had been a busy mining area at one time but the mines must have played out.

As the sun settled behind the western wall of the canyon, Brent reached the spot opposite the ranch house. He had to familiarize himself with the situation here, if he had any hope of getting the girl to leave the canyon with him— the girl Zarada said was here.

Brent knew he couldn't slip out the mouth of the canyon without first getting rid of the guard there. It would certainly be no easy task to get her out past Gunsight Rock and down into that canyon on the other side of the ridge, even if she was willing to go with him. But if he had to kidnap her, his chances were nil, the way he saw it now.

Dusk was deep in the canyon as he moved to the fringe of the aspens where he could see the lighted cabin. There were two men outside the house in the strip of light that spilled through the doorway. He couldn't see their features but they were both big. Then a smaller man came into the light from the direction of the sheep sheds. Several dogs lolled around the door, waiting to be fed.

A medium-sized woman came to the door and said something that brought the men inside. As she stood in the doorway a minute, Brent studied her carefully. She was too far away and the light too dim for him to tell much about her, but he decided she must be the same woman he had seen this afternoon. He was sure she wasn't the girl he was looking for. Something about this woman spoke of age and Virgie Pool was only a week away from her eighteenth birthday.

Brent dug some food out of the sack he had carried over the ridge. He could imagine the hot meal being served inside the ranch house and it did nothing to make his cold bread and meat taste any better. The wind was blowing in the wrong direction for him to catch the smell of the meal in the big log house with the small square windows. He had noted this afternoon that the log house showed none of the expert work of a skilled carpenter and he guessed that Joel Kurtzman and his sons had built the house themselves. It would be shelter enough during the summer, but Brent wondered about its comforts in winter in this high country.

As darkness closed in, Brent ventured closer. He hadn't seen any sign yet of a girl fitting Virgie Pool's description. Could Zarada have been wrong?

He was perhaps halfway between the aspens and the log house when a dog suddenly erupted in a fit of barking on the nearside of the house. For the moment, Brent had forgotten about the half-dozen sheep dogs

Kurtzman kept to handle the sheep. With the sheep safely in the sheds and pens, the dogs were loafing around the house. One of them had caught his scent or heard his approach.

Within ten seconds all the dogs had joined in the uproar. Brent wheeled back to the trees. If the dogs came after him, he'd be in bad trouble. If they were nothing more than sheep dogs, they might stay at the house, their announcement to their masters of someone's approach fulfilling their sense of duty. But if that part-mastiff was among those dogs, he'd follow the intruder, thirsting for the kill. It was in his nature; Brent had seen that this afternoon.

Before Brent reached the trees, he knew that at least one of the dogs was giving chase, maybe more than one. The door of the house had burst open and three men had charged out of the porch. A rifle in one man's hand caught the light streaming through the open door.

Brent reached the trees but he knew he could never outrun those dogs.

CHAPTER FIVE

Emma Kurtzman followed the men as far as the doorway. She had seen them react like this before. Everytime any sign of intrusion into their canyon became evident, they moved like rattler-warned dogs.

'See anything?' Joel demanded, holding his rifle at the ready.

Neither Zeke nor Lud had their rifles, but they were peering into the darkness with the greatest intensity. Zeke, the oldest of the Kurtzman sons, was square built like Joel and strong as a bull. Lud, the second son, was small, weighing fifty pounds less than his brother.

'Ain't nothing in sight,' Zeke said. 'But you can bet something's out there, all right. Old Sandy don't beller like that unless there's a lion or a wolf or a bear after the sheep.'

'Or a strange man,' Joel added, still peering futilely into the dark.

'Ain't no man could get in here,' Lud said. 'Ike's standing guard in the Rocks.'

'He could've gone to sleep,' Joel said. 'Wouldn't be the first time.'

Emma was pushed to one side by her youngest son, Tolly, as he crowded through the doorway to join his father and brothers. It wasn't likely that it was a man out there, Emma reasoned. She hadn't seen a man in this canyon other than her husband, Joel, and her three sons and Ike Starry, their hired hand, since they had come here three years ago.

'Old Sandy didn't sound like he thought it was a lion or a bear,' Zeke speculated.

'He tore out after whatever it is,' Joel agreed. 'He ain't fool enough to go after a lion or bear.'

'Might go after a wolf,' Lud said.

Joel turned to glare at his second son. 'You're scared it'll be a man, ain't you? Afraid you'll be called on to go gunning for him.'

'I don't want to shoot anybody.'

'Any varmint that sneaks in here is marked for shooting, and he knows it before he comes,' Joel said. 'Ain't no crime in giving him what he's asking for.'

Tolly spoke up for the first time, his eyes wild with excitement. 'It's a man, Pa. Let's go get him.'

'How do you know it's a man?' Joel demanded.

'I saw boot tracks up below Gunsight Rock this afternoon,' Tolly said.

'Boots?' Zeke yelled. 'Like them pointed boots cowboys wear?'

Tolly nodded importantly. 'That's what they was.'

Joel grabbed Tolly's shirt front. 'Why didn't you tell us before?'

Tolly's wild eyes widened even farther and he pulled back, cringing as if expecting a blow from Joel. 'Nobody asked me. And any time I say anything, you just say I'm crazy.'

Joel released his grip on Tolly. 'Well, maybe this time you ain't. Zeke, get your rifle. Lud, you, too. We're going to have a look.'

'Should I let Tolliver out?' Tolly asked.

Joel hesitated a moment, then shook his

head. 'No. You and that dog stay here. I don't want that critter with me. He might decide to take off and kill half the sheep—I ought to shoot that dog.'

Tolly surged forward, eyes blazing defiantly. 'Don't you kill Tolliver! He's the best dog that ever lived.'

Joel didn't say anything and Emma stepped up beside Tolly, putting an arm around his shoulders. 'Pa didn't mean it, Tolly. He wouldn't kill Tolliver.'

Joel swore softly and waited till Zeke and Lud came out on the porch with their rifles. Then they stepped off the porch and the darkness swallowed them almost immediately.

'Let's go back inside and wait,' Emma suggested gently to Tolly.

She went back into the living room and Tolly followed. The supper dishes were still on the table; in fact, the plates weren't all cleaned up. That presented a problem for Emma. If she cleaned up the supper table and Joel and the boys came back right away to finish their supper, Joel would raise Old Ned because she hadn't kept supper hot for them. On the other hand, if she left the table set and Joel wasn't hungry when he got in, he'd rave like a thunderstorm on the peaks because she hadn't done her work.

She made a quick decision. 'Let's clean it up, Virgie,' she said to the girl who had obediently stayed inside during all the furor.

Joel's first order when the dogs started barking had been for Virgie to stay in the house.

Virgie was short like all the Kurtzmans but there the similarity to her brothers disappeared. Virgie had auburn, almost red hair and blue eyes. All three of Emma's sons had Emma's black eyes and all had hair either black or so dark brown it looked black. Virgie didn't have the blocky build of the Kurtzmans, either. Except for Tolly, none of Emma's men was over five feet nine but Joel and Zeke each weighed over two hundred pounds. Virgie didn't weight much over a hundred.

'Why wouldn't Pa let me go with him?' Tolly grumbled. 'I can shoot a rifle as well as he can. And I ain't afraid to shoot a man, either, like Lud is.'

'It isn't likely that a man's out there, Tolly,' Emma explained softly. 'Besides, three of them are enough to find whoever or whatever it is.'

Emma was more concerned about her youngest son than any of the others. She felt pity for Tolly whose mind had not been right since Joel had beaten him one day for running away when he was barely five years old. Somehow Tolly's head had been hurt. He had never been right since. Emma had come nearer hating Joel that day than ever before or since. She was sure that Joel had regretted his act afterward, but when his anger was hot, he had no restraint.

With the table cleared, Emma turned to the stove to get the teakettle of hot water to begin washing dishes. Virgie got the dish towel to dry them. Watching the girl, Emma thought that she couldn't possibly have thought more of her own daughter than she did of Virgie. Of course, Virgie didn't know that she wasn't Emma's daughter. And it hadn't been until about three years ago that Emma had suspected that Virgie was anything more than the waif that Joel had said he'd found out on the prairie and brought home because there was no place else to take her.

For weeks Emma had waited expectantly for someone to come and claim the little girl. And each day her hopes had grown stronger that no one would. She had three sons then but no daughter. Little Virgie filled a void in her life. Virgie was a little older than Tolly, Emma's youngest, but when it became apparent that no one was going to claim the little girl, Emma gave Virgie Tolly's birthday. Both Virgie and Tolly thought that Tolly was exactly one year younger than she was and they celebrated their birthdays together.

Emma had brought up her family out on the Colorado-Utah border where they had few neighbors and even fewer friends. Joel had seen to that. Then about three years ago, they had moved back to the eastern slope of the Rockies and located in Gunsight Canyon and began raising sheep. Emma knew that Joel had

44

spread the word that he had a son who was a bit off in the head and he was holing up in this canyon so that the authorities wouldn't try to take Tolly away from them.

But Emma had begun to piece things together bit by bit as she realized that Joel had never told her all the truth about things. And the picture she saw as the puzzle fit together both shocked and horrified her.

It was Joel's repeated warnings that Virgie must never go outside the canyon that first roused Emma's suspicions. She could understand why Tolly wouldn't be allowed outside the canyon. But why Virgie? She was perfectly sane, and pretty as a picture to Emma's way of thinking. Maybe Joel didn't want any suitors coming around to call, for fear they would report Tolly's condition. Fat chance they'd have of getting into the canyon if they tried, the way Joel kept it guarded day and night.

As Virgie grew prettier every day, Emma began to worry about another thing. Zeke and Lud had both been old enough when Joel brought Virgie home to know that she was not their real sister. Joel had almost beaten Zeke senseless one day when he said something that Virgie could have interpreted as meaning she wasn't a Kurtzman. But she hadn't understood, and Joel made certain nothing was ever said again that would let the secret out.

Zeke was twenty-two now and he didn't get outside the canyon much. How long would it be before Zeke decided it was time he let Virgie know she wasn't his sister and began courting her like he would some pretty girl down on the plains? Emma wouldn't stand for it, that's all. Zeke was her own son but he just wasn't good enough for Virgie. He was as mean and vicious as Joel, and Emma had learned long ago just how mean and vicious that was.

Lud was a different matter. It was as if he'd been plucked out of another family and set down here. Ordinarily he was a gentle boy. If Joel hadn't prodded him to be as hard and tough as his older brother, Lud would have been the gentle dreamer that Nature had intended him to be. He wasn't big enough to be a tough hand battler, anyway, and he hated to shoot at anything living. But Joel goaded him until he almost lost his mind. When he was pushed too far, he was liable to do almost anything. It was at those moments that Emma, who usually thought of Lud as a beautiful child, was almost afraid of him.

Tolly was her prime concern, however. He was a couple of inches taller than Zeke but not as heavy. Only seventeen, he might fill out like Zeke some day. If he did, he'd be a big man and with his child's mind, he would be dangerous. Joel would never consent to having Tolly put some place where he couldn't harm anyone, but Emma knew the day might come when it would have to be done.

Tolly was almost always gentle around Emma or Virgie. In fact, he was the only one of her brothers that Virgie really trusted, Emma thought. Both Tolly and Virgie were afraid of Joel. Even Emma had moments when she was afraid of him. His temper could be monumental. Tolly stayed away from him whenever he could. He never opposed him unless he thought his dog, Tolliver, was in danger. Tolly would face death without flinching to save his dog from a beating.

'Ma, you've stopped washing the dishes. What's wrong?'

Emma jerked her thoughts back to the dishpan in front of her. She hadn't realized she had stopped working while her mind wandered.

'I was thinking of Pa and the boys out there looking for something that they can't see,' she said. 'Could be dangerous.'

'They can take care of themselves,' Virgie said confidently. 'They don't have to back off from anything.'

Emma nodded without answering. How right Virgie was! Joel, especially, was self-sufficient. Emma hadn't learned until she got to Gunsight Canyon that Joel had once been in prison. He had never even hinted of such a thing to her. But shortly after they arrived here, Joel had brought Ike Starry home with him and announced that he would be staying and helping with the work on the ranch.

Emma hadn't liked Starry but she hadn't objected. Joel could use help with all the sheep he planned to run in the canyon. But Starry got some whiskey one day and it loosened his tongue. He told Emma that he and Joel had been in prison together years ago and had escaped together. Then, not long ago, Starry had robbed a stagecoach and Joel had found him before the law did. He had threatened to turn him in to the law unless he came here and helped herd sheep. Starry hated sheep but he hated prison worse. So he stayed in the canyon, never going outside. It was a perfect hideout for him.

Emma finished the dishes and left Virgie to put them away while she went out on the porch to enjoy the cool breeze and wait for her men to come back. Tolly sulked in the corner of the living room, angry because Joel hadn't let him and Tolliver go on the hunt, too. The truth was, Emma thought, that Joel was afraid of Tolliver. Zeke had brought the pup home to Tolly, but it had been Joel who had named him, giving the dog the same name as his son. Emma believed Joel hated them both and maybe was a bit afraid of them both. Tolly didn't realize that his dog had the same name as he did because he'd always been called Tolly and the dog was called Tolliver.

The breeze whispered through the canyon

as Emma dropped into the big rocker that always stood on the porch. She stared off into the darkness, listening for sounds. There was none, other than the little creek rippling by. The men were either too far from the house for any sound to carry back, or else they had located something and were silently stalking it. Joel had taught his boys well how to stalk an animal or an enemy. She wondered which this was tonight.

As she watched and waited, her mind dropped back to a problem that had nagged her since she had learned about Joel's prison sentence and escape. Just before they had moved from their first home to the Utah-Colorado border, Joel had been gone for a few days. He had told her only that he had a job to do, and he had been very upset and irritable before he left. When he came back, he had brought the little girl, Virgie. Shortly after that, they had moved across the mountains.

Emma had heard some shocking things before they left but she saw no connection between them and Joel until after they returned to the eastern slope and her memory dredged up these events. She had heard of the ambushing of the young man who owned the fine ranch along Bitter Creek, and of the accident that caused the death of his wife and daughter the next day. She had tried to forget that tragedy when they moved away.

Then, after they returned, Starry had told

her about Joel's prison life and his escape. Things began dropping into place, and fitting too well. Joel had been gone from home exactly when the man and his family were killed. And he had brought home a little girl. What she didn't know was whether that man's little girl had actually been killed. If she had, then her suspicions of Joel would be lifted.

That had plagued her for a year after Starry came to the canyon. Then she had decided to find out. Against Joel's orders and without his knowledge, she made arrangements with Lud, who was guarding the canyon mouth that day, to let her through and not say anything about it. It had been a long ride for her to get to Jubilee, the home town of the Pool ranch, but she made it even though she wasn't used to riding much. What she learned there that day was an eye-opener.

The Pool girl was declared dead by most people but her body had never been found—just some of her clothes in the wreck. Neither the man who had killed Henry Pool nor the one who had caused the wreck, if it hadn't been an accident, had ever been found.

She recognized some people in town she had known over fifteen years ago. One, Jarron Dix, had recognized her, too, and had asked her a lot of questions about Joel. She had answered evasively, and left town as quickly as possible but she had wondered if Dix suspected Joel as she did.

Emma had hoped to slip back into the canyon without Joel knowing she was gone. But he had missed her and was waiting at the canyon mouth for her. When she told him she had gone to town, he tried to beat her to death but she had not submitted docilely to his beating and fought back. Her spirited defense conquered Joel's raging temper and she began demanding answers from him. He finally broke down and told her the whole story, threatening to kill her if she ever told anyone.

Emma had no intention of telling anyone. In fact, she had no intention of ever doing anything that would break up her family, and if this became common knowledge, she would certainly lose Virgie as well as Joel. Joel wouldn't say who had forced him to ambush Henry Pool or run his wife's buggy over the cliff, but she suspected it was Jarron Dix. Dix evidently knew about Joel's escape from prison and gave Joel the choice of doing this job for him or going back to prison. It couldn't have been an easy choice for Joel.

Emma still wasn't sure that Joel had told her everything. He had insisted that Virgie had to be kept out of sight; at least, until after her eighteenth birthday, which he said was the twentieth of June. Emma didn't know whether he knew that was the date or was guessing. And he wouldn't tell her the reason for keeping her out of sight until she was eighteen. She now wondered if it could have anything to do with the tracks of a man Tolly had said he'd seen a week ago up by Gunsight Rock. And then Tolly had said he'd seen boot tracks up there today. This was the thirteenth of June. A week from today Virgie would be eighteen, if Joel was right about the date of her birthday.

With a perplexed sigh, Emma got up and went back inside. Joel and the two boys might be out all night if Joel thought there really was a stranger in the canyon. He'd just keep after him till he got him and there would be another killing.

Emma had gone to bed when the men came in. Joel would only grunt when she asked him what they found. Knowing Joel, she decided they hadn't found anything, but he wasn't convinced that the dogs hadn't heard something.

Breakfast was before daylight. At the first crack of light in the canyon, Joel sent Zeke out to look for tracks. Was it a man or a lion or a bear? Whatever it was it had to leave tracks. Lud was sent down to the mouth of the canyon to relieve Ike Starry and he went with Joel's warning that he'd be horsewhipped if he let anyone past him, either in or out of the canyon.

Emma had to get another breakfast for Ike Starry when he came in a half hour after sunup. He was bleary-eyed from lack of sleep and that didn't help his appearance any.

Emma was sure nothing could make him attractive. He was about the same age as Joel with a straggly beard that he never combed. His beady eyes seemed to be set back in his head almost out of sight. When Joel questioned him about the night before, he grunted his answers while he gulped his food. He had heard nothing and seen nothing.

While Starry headed for his bunk in the back room, Joel got his rifle and went to the door. Tolly grabbed his rifle and followed.

'I'm going, too, Pa,' Tolly said before Joel could object. 'Tolliver can track a gnat through a creek. He'll find whoever's out there.'

Joel appeared ready to order Tolly to stay at the house but he changed his mind. Instead, he turned to Virgie and shook a finger at her.

'You stay indoors every daylit minute. If you have to go outside, make it fast and don't let anybody see you. Don't talk to nobody but one of the family.'

'Who else would I see in this canyon?' Virgie asked.

'Somebody or something is in the canyon that doesn't belong here. If you see a stranger, you hightail it back to the house. Understand?'

Emma thought Virgie was going to ask why and she knew that would bring an explosion from Joel. Virgie apparently knew it, too, and held back the question. She looked at Emma and Emma nodded. She had to agree with Joel. If anybody saw Virgie, it might mean that

Virgie would be taken from her and Emma didn't think she could stand that. Virgie was all that made life here in the canyon bearable.

She watched Joel's grim face as he left the house. Joel was sure there was a man in the canyon and Emma didn't wonder what the man wanted—it had to be Virgie. But what would he do if he found her? Icy fingers seemed to squeeze a band around her heart. She hoped Joel found the man before he found Virgie.

CHAPTER SIX

Brent Clark had no illusions about what would happen to him if the Kurtzmans found him. Zarada had warned him that Joel Kurtzman would kill him on sight. He considered his escape from the men last night almost a miracle. The dogs that had given away his presence had started toward him but had been sidetracked by some scent they ran across in the grass, probably a coyote or bobcat. They had followed that scent, acting like anything but shepherds. Brent wondered if there wasn't some hunting blood in all of Kurtzman's dogs.

Brent had faded back into the aspens and watched three men leave the light at the house. Clouds had filtered over the canyon since the sun had gone down, blocking out the

54

light from the sky. Brent couldn't see the men but he could hear them, even though they were moving very quietly. They followed the dogs.

Brent had moved back to the wall of the canyon and found a mine shaft that opened almost on a level with the valley floor. Feeling his way back inside the tunnel, he settled down, listening for sounds of the dogs or men, but he heard neither and eventually he slept.

Daylight sifted down into the canyon, arriving late at the mine where Brent was because it was on the east side of the canyon. He awoke with stabbing hunger pangs. He opened the sack he had filled at Zarada's and took out some bread and meat. He thought of building a fire and boiling some coffee in the little pan in his sack but he was afraid to risk the fire. The smell of smoke would hang for a long time in the still air of the canyon.

After dulling his hunger, he found a rock ledge like a shelf back a little deeper in the mine and put his sack there. It wasn't the safest place to store it but he couldn't carry it with him all the time. He made sure he had plenty of ammunition in his pockets for both his rifle and revolver then left the cave and moved through the aspens to a spot where he could see the valley.

There was activity near the house and as Brent kept out of sight, he still managed to see a man and the boy he'd almost run into up near Gunsight Rock yesterday leave the house.

The big dog was at the boy's side. They went toward the mouth of the canyon and Brent waited until they were out of sight before moving.

He guessed that at least one man was guarding the mouth of the canyon. Zarada had said there were three sons but he didn't say how many hired hands. So there was at least one son and perhaps a hired man or two that Brent couldn't account for. He decided that none of them were at the house, though, because the sheep were still locked in their pens. Apparently Joel Kurtzman had been so upset he hadn't been able to find what had triggered off the dogs' barking last night that he had gone off this morning without turning the sheep out to pasture.

Brent's job now was to contact Virgie somehow, if she was here. He had to try to convince her who she really was and how important it was for her to get out of the canyon and show up at Greeley for the estate settlement. Brent wanted to be out of this canyon by noon today if possible. Since the man and the boy had gone down the canyon, this might be his best chance.

Looking over the area, he located a place downstream where trees and bushes grew along the waterway and the stream cut at an angle across the floor of the canyon. If Brent followed the aspens down to a spot opposite the bend in the stream, he would have only a short open space to cross before finding cover again in the serviceberry bushes along the creek. Then he could follow the stream up to the buildings. Virgie would surely be in or near that house, if she was here at all, Brent thought again.

When he ran across the open space between the aspens and the stream, he felt as exposed as he had yesterday on that slope above the plains. If anybody above or below saw him, they'd know he was an intruder from the way he moved, especially since he was several inches taller than any of the Kurtzmans and not as squarely built. There would be no point in trying to pass himself off as one of them making the crossing to the stream.

Once in the bushes, he found he had to drop down to the edge of the stream itself to find walking room. Pines were scattered along the stream bank but the serviceberry bushes were like a thicket. At times he was actually wading in the edge of the stream but he lost little time in getting up near the buildings. There he stopped, uncertain about his next move. Very likely at least one man was at the house to protect the women, especially Virgie, if Joel Kurtzman had guessed that the intruder was here to steal the girl.

The decision was taken out of his hands, however, when he saw a girl come out of the house along with an older woman. The woman was protesting something but the girl was softly arguing her point, and apparently won it. She stepped off the porch and skipped down to the sheep pens.

Brent guessed what she was going to do. The men had neglected to turn out the sheep so she was going to do it. The dogs followed her eagerly.

Brent had seen the ford just above the house. There was a narrow wooden bridge over the stream at this place and all the brush had been cut away. That little bridge would be for the sheep to cross the creek. They wouldn't wade the stream unless absolutely forced to. A creek was as good as a fence for holding sheep.

Brent slipped back into the edge of the stream and hurried ahead almost to the ford. There he moved back into the serviceberry bushes and waited. He heard the sheep coming and he hoped the dogs wouldn't scent him. He doubted if they would with the dust and the heavy sheep smell filling the air.

The first sheep hit the bridge and trotted across, following in single file by all the sheep from the pens. The bridge rattled for several minutes before the last of the sheep were across. A couple of the dogs followed the sheep over the bridge while the rest splashed across the stream and moved the sheep toward the grazing grounds up the canyon.

The girl followed the last dog across the bridge and stood at the other end watching the dogs handle the sheep. Apparently satisfied that they were going to be all right, she turned and started back across the bridge toward the house.

Brent held his breath as he got a straight look at the girl. Her eyes were as blue as the morning sky above the canyon and her auburn hair hung down her back almost to her hips. It had been combed but hadn't been rolled up for the day and it shone like red gold. She was small, scarcely five feet tall and so slim it seemed that a puff of wind might blow her away. Her face, however, was not so thin and her rosy cheeks accented her rather short nose and red lips.

Brent hardly realized that he had stood up close to the bridge. She didn't see him at first, her eyes on the water rippling under the bridge. When she did see him, she stopped and gasped, almost falling off the bridge.

'Don't be scared,' Brent said softly. 'I'm not going to hurt you. I just want to talk to you.'

She shook her head violently and looked toward the house. To get there, she'd have to walk very close to Brent. For a moment, he thought she was going to jump off into the water and go around him. Then she turned her eyes back to him, fear in them but defiance, too, like a cornered animal.

'Your name is Virgie, isn't it?' he asked, crowding closer to the bridge.

She backed off a step and nodded, not

taking her eyes off him.

'Do you remember the name Virgie Pool? Or Virginia Pool?'

She simply stared at him and he wondered if the name Pool even rang a faint bell in her memory. The fear in her eyes covered any other emotion that might have tried to come through.

'Do your remember when you were a little girl, Virginia?'

She started to nod her head, then shook it instead. She wasn't going to talk and the foolish thought ran through his mind that he'd rather hear her voice right now than any sound in the world. Maybe her voice would be as pretty as her face. Seeing Virgie here in this canyon was like finding a wild rose in a patch of sunflowers.

Suddenly, with a burst of speed that caught him entirely by surprise, she darted past him and ran toward the house. He looked after her but his attention was snatched away by the bellow of a dog back down the canyon. Brent didn't need to be told that was Tolly's mastiff. He must have found the scent of Brent down along the creek. He'd be coming up this creek swiftly now.

Brent vaulted over the little bridge and ran across the bare strip that had been cleared for the ford. Again diving into the serviceberry bushes on the far side of the ford, he ran upstream. He wasn't sure where he was going.

He stepped into the creek and ran in the water, hoping to throw the dog off his scent.

Feeling like the escaped slaves must have felt with bloodhounds on their trails, he splashed ahead, looking for a place where he could hide. The mastiff might even have some bloodhound in him.

After that first bellow, there had been no other sound but Brent wasn't foolish enough to believe the dog had lost his trail. Maybe Tolly had him on a leash which would slow him some.

The creek turned and twisted much more than he remembered from looking down on it yesterday. Now when he wanted to make as good time as possible and still keep out of sight, it seemed that the stream wandered like a drunken man.

Suddenly he came around a bend in the creek and stopped short. He was face to face with the grinning boy, Tolly, and the huge dog. Tolly had his rifle cocked and pointed straight at him. The dog was on a tight leash fastened to the boy's belt.

'Figured you was trying to run in the water to keep old Tolliver from smelling you out,' the boy said.

Brent sized up the situation instantly. He was caught. And that wild look in the boy's eyes warned him not to make any false move or he'd be dead.

'This'll make Pa sit up and take notice of

me,' Tolly said excitedly. 'He's been hunting the whole canyon for you, and ain't seen hide nor hair of you. I'll show him that me and Tolliver can beat him tracking.'

'What do you figure on doing with me?' Brent asked as calmly as possible.

'Shoot you, I reckon,' Tolly said grinning. 'Pa said nobody is to come into our canyon and live to get out.'

Brent's mind was racing. There was no way of predicting what a crazy boy like Tolly might do. Brent didn't doubt that Tolly could kill him and think he'd done a wonderful thing.

'You want to make a good impression on your pa?' Brent asked slowly.

'Sure, And this'll do it. When I drag your carcass into the yard, he'll know I'm a better man than either one of my brothers.'

'Doesn't he treat you as well as them?'

Tolly frowned. 'No, he sure don't. But he will now.'

'Maybe you ought to use me as a bargaining point with your pa,' Brent said.

Tolly stared at Brent. 'Seeing you dead is all the bargaining I need.'

Brent shook his head. 'That won't help you any. But if you keep me a prisoner some place where your pa can't find me, you can demand anything from your pa and get it. Just tell him you'll turn me loose again if he mistreats you.'

A new light suddenly fired Tolly's eyes. 'Hey, that's a good idea. Pa won't like it, but he'll have to be good to me as long as I've got you tied up somewhere. Boy, will I make Pa toe the line!'

Brent realized that he had scored a point with Tolly. It was likely Tolly could be talked into almost anything. Joel Kurtzman probably would make him tell where he had Brent imprisoned. But this ruse had postponed Brent's death for a little while, anyway.

'Toss your rifle over on the bank,' Tolly ordered. 'Then your six-gun.'

Brent did as he was told. For the moment, he was safe from Tolly's rifle. He couldn't risk losing that advantage by hesitating to obey his orders even for an instant. Tolly moved over and got the rifle and revolver, leaving the dog on a longer leash to watch Brent. Neither Brent nor the dog moved, but the dog's eyes never left Brent and a growl rumbled in his throat almost constantly. Brent could almost feel the dog's desire to leap at his throat.

'Move out ahead of me,' Tolly ordered. 'I know just the place to put you where nobody will find you.'

Tolly marched Brent up the canyon, still keeping close to the creek. That was to keep his father and brothers from seeing him, Brent guessed. If they saw where he took him, then Tolly's bargaining power would be gone.

They passed the sheep off to the left and Tolliver growled ominously. Tolly jerked on the leash and he quieted down. They moved past the sheep and were well into the upper end of the canyon when Tolly directed Brent to turn toward the west wall. Pine trees were scattered over the area where they left the little creek and soon they came to a stand of aspens close to the canyon wall.

Moving through these, Tolly directed Brent up a steep trail that climbed over the tailings of a mine, the opening of which was almost hidden by a couple of small trees that had grown up since the mine was abandoned. Brent was shoved behind these trees and into the mine.

It was very dark inside, the trees shutting out most of the natural light. Tolly got a match from a box on a rock just inside the tunnel mouth and struck it, then lighted a candle that was on the rock. Brent realized that this must be a secret hiding place of Tolly's. He probably didn't think any of his family knew about it. Brent hoped they didn't.

'Move on to the back end,' Tolly ordered.

Brent kept walking with Tolly right behind him with the candle. Finally Tolly called a halt and set the candle on another rock. Brent could see in the flickering light a tree stump that was evidently used for a chair and a knife that had been used for whittling. There was also a pile of rope and Tolly picked that up now.

He backed Brent against a supporting pole holding up the roof of the mine and made him sit down. Then he began lashing the rope around Brent and the pole. Brent began thinking about how he would get this rope off even before Tolly finished tying it. Tolly worked quite a while behind Brent before he was satisfied.

'That'll do it,' Tolly said finally with satisfaction, picking up the candle. 'I'm going to tell Pa off now. I'll get some respect from him.'

He carried the candle back to the rock at the opening and blew it out. The odor from the extinguished candle drifted back to Brent. But there was no sound or other smell in the tunnel except the dank odor of damp rocks.

As soon as Tolly was gone, Brent began working on the ropes, trying to get a hand free. But the boy had done a good job of tying the ropes. Every move Brent made seemed to draw the ropes tighter.

After ten minutes of frantic working, Brent realized he couldn't get loose. He had talked himself into a corner. The only way that Tolly would ever untie him would be if he shot him first. Tolly knew that his father wanted him dead and he intended to please his father in the hope of earning some respect.

Suddenly Brent thought of another possibility. This pole he was tied to was a brace in the mine. Maybe he could jerk the pole loose from its moorings and then he could work the ropes off.

He jerked his body forward with all his strength. The pole gave an inch and a shower of dirt cascaded down from the ceiling. Brent gritted his teeth and gave the pole another jerk. Again it yielded a little, but this time two big chunks of rock fell from the ceiling. Brent wished he could see up there. It seemed that the pole really was holding up the ceiling.

He gave the pole another jerk, easier this time. A shower of rocks fell from the ceiling and he heard a crack as if another rock or the pole itself had split. He sat quietly as the dust slowly settled. That dust and rock shower had lasted for half a minute. He knew he had almost brought the ceiling down. He dare not wiggle that pole any more or he would be buried under tons of rocks.

He sat quietly, trying to think of some way out of his dilemma. The only conclusion he could reach was that he was at the complete mercy of a crazy boy.

Tolly came back sometime much later. Brent had no way of telling what time it was. The darkness this far back in the mine was almost total. He heard the boy and dog at the mouth of the tunnel, then he saw the candle being lit. Tolly came back to Brent. He looked at the rocks lying around.

'I see you've been trying to jerk that pole down. I forgot to tell you that if you pull that pole loose, this whole mine will cave in. Then I won't have any live bait to tease Pa with. So you be careful.'

'How about something to eat?' Brent asked.

Tolly looked at Brent and shrugged. 'Why should I waste any grub on you? You're dead, anyway. Don't you know that?'

Brent hunched forward and a little shower of dust fell. The dog moved ahead an inch, growling eagerly. Only Tolly's restraining hand on his leash held him back.

'Like I said, you move too much and you'll be buried alive,' Tolly repeated. 'Now you keep quiet till I make Pa admit I'm as good as Zeke or Lud.'

Turning, he dragged the dog after him to the tunnel mouth, blew out the candle, and left.

Brent sat still in the darkness. He had talked himself into more trouble than if he'd let Tolly shoot him back there at the creek or drag him up to the house to face Joel and the other Kurtzmans. Even if he didn't make a wrong move and bring the ceiling down, he'd soon starve to death here. That crazy boy wasn't going to feed him.

CHAPTER SEVEN

Virgie was glad that her father and brothers hadn't been at the house when she encountered the stranger at the bridge. They surely would have seen him and killed him. Or if he'd gotten away, they'd have trailed him till they caught him and then killed him. She didn't like killing, even of an enemy.

He hadn't seemed to be the demon that her father and brothers claimed but appearances could be deceiving. He was about the first stranger she had seen since they came back from the west slope three years ago. She didn't know how to judge anyone except by comparison with her father or her brothers. Of course, there was Ike Starry, but he was so repulsive in his appearance and manners that she couldn't think of him in the same moment with the stranger.

Ike was at the house now, but he'd be asleep. She'd seen him come in almost every morning when he had been on night watch at the canyon entrance. He'd gulp down his breakfast, then head for the little lean-to on the house where he seemed to begin snoring almost before he hit his bed.

Only her mother could have seen the stranger this morning. She had been working in the kitchen and, but unless she had looked out the window at just the right time, she probably hadn't seen him either. Somehow, Virgie hoped no one had seen him. She had to be afraid of him; Joel had said that anyone who would sneak into their canyon was an outlaw, worse than a thief. He had never said it right out, but she got the idea that he thought any man coming into the canyon would be after her. She'd stay away from the stranger, even though she secretly hoped that Joel and her brothers didn't find him.

It was quiet around the house; it always was, it seemed. Virgie and her mother had little to talk about and the men were usually gone. Ike Starry snored away in the lean-to. She doubted if an earthquake would wake him. The dogs were out with the sheep. Those sheep gave Virgie about the only excuse she had for getting out of the house. Someone had to check frequently to make sure the dogs were keeping the sheep in the upper end of the valley.

An hour after she had turned the sheep out of the pens, Virgie started toward the door to go out and check them. With Joel and Zeke and Tolly out looking for the stranger in the valley, Emma might not let her step outside. She wouldn't if she knew that Virgie had seen the man. But Emma didn't know, and she didn't stop her from going outside and up on the rock west of the cabin; from which the entire upper valley was visible.

From the top of the rock, she shaded her eyes against the sun. The sheep were in the right area and the dogs were lying around, apparently asleep, but aware of where the sheep were. She turned to look down the canyon. Trees blocked much of the view in that direction, but there was no sign of Joel or Zeke or Tolly down there. They had gone that way this morning looking for the stranger.

Turning back to the upper end of the canyon, she gazed lovingly at the spire at the end of the canyon. She had been allowed to go up there once or twice when there seemed to be no danger in the valley. She loved the view of the canyon from there, and she wondered what she would see if she could go just a little farther and look down into the canyon beyond. This had become home and she loved it. But, there was the nagging question as to what lay beyond. This canyon couldn't hold her forever. She knew that, but she had no idea how she would ever break out of it or what rude surprises might await her if she did.

Suddenly her eyes focused on a figure coming down the creek. To anyone not used to seeing every tree and rock in place along the creek, he might not have been visible. But Virgie had everthing memorized. Any movement or any figure that wasn't part of the permanent picture was bound to catch her eye.

Her first thought was that it was the stranger. Then she recognized the odd, loping run of Tolly. What was he doing up in that end of the canyon? He had gone toward the mouth, along with Joel.

Instead of going back to the house, Virgie waited on the rock. Tolly was coming toward the house. She'd ask him a few questions. He'd talk to her. He wasn't so free with words with his father or brothers.

Tolly loped into sight from the trees along the creek, reaching the bridge and turning up the road toward the buildings. Virgie slid off the rock and intercepted him before he got to the house.

'What were you doing up-canyon?' she asked.

Tolly grinned knowingly, and Virgie surmised he'd been up to something he considered brilliant. 'Caught me a varmint,' he said.

'A wolf or a bear cub?' Virgie asked frowning.

'Better than that,' Tolly said delightedly. 'A two-legged varmint.'

'The stranger?' she asked unbelievingly.

Tolly nodded. 'But don't you go telling Pa. I want to tell him.'

'Pa'll kill him!' Virgie said.

'Not till he admits I'm as smart as Zeke or Lud,' Tolly said. 'I got him hid where nobody can find him.'

Virgie's mind was racing. She was surprised that Tolly had thought of this scheme to blackmail Joel. Tolly didn't usually think of anything more complicated than stalking game or getting what he wanted to eat and wear. She had a good idea where the stranger was hidden. She had trailed Tolly to his hideout in the mine. So far as she knew, though, she was the only member of the family who knew about Tolly's hideout. He guarded his secret with vicious jealousy.

'How long will you keep him hidden?' Virgie asked then, a new thought plaguing her. She had seen the little birds and animals that Tolly had caught. Invariably, he had refused to feed them and they starved to death. He'd do the same with a man.

'I'll keep him there till Pa admits I'm smart enough to go outside the canyon like Zeke and Lud,' Tolly said. 'That's how long.'

'What'll you feed him?'

'Don't have to feed him,' Tolly said. 'Pa's going to kill him, anyway. No sense in wasting good grub on something that's as good as dead.'

'This is a man, Tolly. You can't let a man starve. That would be murder and you don't want to be a murderer.'

'Pa would do it. Why can't I?'

That was a question Virgie couldn't answer on the spur of the moment. Tolly wanted to please Joel so that Joel would treat him as an equal to his brothers. If he thought Joel would kill the stranger, then he couldn't see any reason why he should try to keep him alive. Nothing Virgie could say would change his mind.

Tolly went on toward the house, and Virgie turned to took up the canyon. She was amazed that in spite of the way Joel mistreated his sons, especially Tolly and Lud, that they continued to try so hard to please him. Yet, Virgie was also aware that was the only course left open to them. Locked in this canyon, they had to get along with Joel.

Tolly was a prisoner here in this canyon, never allowed to go outside. It was natural that he'd do anything he could to negotiate the privilege to get outside. She was as much a prisoner as Tolly was, but she knew there was no way she could negotiate the right to get outside. This canyon, as beautiful as it was, was a prison for the entire Kurtzman family, including Joel. He was the jailor and his responsibility in keeping those inside from getting out, and anyone outside from getting in, must bear heavily on him.

Virgie had spent hours speculating on Joel's reason for keeping this canyon, and everything in it, shut off completely from the outside world. His excuse that he had to prevent anyone from seeing Tolly in order to keep him out of an institution, might carry some weight so far as Tolly was concerned, but it didn't include her. She wasn't mentally incompetent. In fact, she had a better education than any member of the family. While they were on the western slope, she had attended school regularly until she was fifteen. Neither Joel nor Emma or any of the boys could read very well. The ability to read and write was held in very low esteem in the Kurtzman household. Virgie had been allowed to go to school because Joel didn't consider girls worth anything—he had let her go to get her out of the way.

She wandered slowly back toward the house. If she didn't come in soon, Emma would come looking for her. Virgie had a real love for her mother. Emma did everything for her that a mother could do under the circumstances. Emma had stood between her and Joel's wrath more than once, although it was clear that she was sometimes as afraid of Joel as Virgie and Tolly were.

She thought of asking Emma to help the stranger, but abandoned that idea immediately. Emma had seemed as eager to get rid of the stranger as Joel had although Virgie couldn't think it was for the same reason. Joel seemed to want to kill anyone who trespassed in his valley, as did Zeke, Joel's carbon copy.

But Lud was different. He didn't have the lust to kill that dominated both Joel and Zeke. He liked to read and write poetry, although he knew better than to let anyone except Virgie know it. No one else, in fact, knew he wrote them, and she wouldn't have known if she hadn't stumbled onto him one day in the grove out by the pasture laboriously writing some poetry. He barely had enough education to write, but it wasn't his fault. He wanted to go to school but after four terms, Joel said he had enough book learning to be a man.

Lud tried to be as mean and vicious as Zeke to please Joel, but he couldn't do it. And what was even worse was that he couldn't hide his gentle nature from Joel. Virgie thought that Joel almost hated Lud because of that. If there was a nasty job to do, he gave it to Lud. And he forced Lud into situations where he had to be brutal to survive.

Joel and Zeke came in for dinner, disgusted and angry. They hadn't found the intruder, but they were convinced that he hadn't left the canyon. They had found tracks proving that someone besides the Kurtzmans was here. Virgie watched Tolly, but he was smart enough to know that was not the time to try to get any concessions from Joel. He ate with his head buried in his plate, not taking any part in the conversation. For the moment, the stranger was safe from Joel, Virgie thought.

The afternoon brought no further clues to the location of the stranger, and Joel was beginning to doubt that he was still in the canyon. Ike Starry was sent out to relieve Lud as guard at the canyon mouth. Again Joel gave him the explicit instructions to watch that nobody slipped out of or into the canyon.

Virgie lay awake an hour after going to bed, thinking of the stranger. He must be hungry now. There was no telling what kind of shape Tolly had left him in. He might be tied up so that his blood couldn't circulate properly. Tolly wouldn't think of that or care if he did think of it. When morning came, Virgie resolved to take some food to the man. A tingle of excitement ran over her, something like the time she had faced a young mountain lion to protect the sheep. Danger put a sweet taste in her mouth like the tang of a crispy apple. She would be in danger taking food to the stranger; if not from the stranger himself, then from Joel or Zeke, or even Tolly, if they found out about it.

While she was cleaning up the table after breakfast, she slipped some of the food into a flour sack that Emma kept stored in the cupboard against the day when she would need another dish towel. She managed to get something besides scraps, for there was some set back for Ike Starry when he came in for his late breakfast after Lud relieved him for the day watch. Ike just wouldn't have as much to eat as usual. She hoped he wouldn't notice. He was usually too tired to know what he was doing. He always seemed to be tired.

Slipping the sack into her room, she waited until Ike had gulped his breakfast, grumbled a bit about not having enough, then went off to

76

the lean-to and dropped into bed. While Emma was cleaning the top of the stove, Virgie slipped out the door, the sack tucked in front of her where Emma wouldn't see it. Joel and Zeke had left already, still hunting the stranger. Tolly had been gone for a while too. Virgie worried that he might be at the mine when she got there. She didn't dare let him see her. She got along fine with Tolly, but if she interfered with his scheme, he could be vicious.

She went out past the big rock and, using it to guard her from sight of the house, moved away until she was in some trees. From there, she slipped down to the creek and started upstream. She was almost even with Tolly's hideout when she saw Tolly coming down from the mine toward the creek.

She sank down into the grass and bushes near the trees and waited, hoping he wouldn't see her. Tolly came down the little path that led from the tree blocking the view of the tunnel mouth. As Tolly and his dog passed close to Virgie, Tolliver growled deep in his throat. Tolly stopped, and looked at the dog. But when he spoke to him, the dog turned away and Tolly went on. Apparently, the dog had identified Virgie and knew there was no danger from that source.

With Tolly and his dog out of sight, Virgie hurried up the path to the tree and slipped past it into the mine. Her former visit here had acquainted her with the candle Tolly kept at the entrance. She found the matches and lit the candle, making her way back into the mine. She had no idea how far back the stranger would be.

She was almost on Brent before she saw him. He was staring at her without moving. Virgie almost dropped her candle. Then she saw that he was bound and she sat the candle on a rock and opened the sack of food.

'You're going to feed me?' the stranger asked in surprise.

'Tolly won't,' she said. 'You'll die.'

'I believe that,' he said.

She considered untying his hands so he could eat by himself but decided against it. This was the man Joel and Zeke and Lud were looking for. She remembered even Emma was hoping they would catch him and get rid of him. She shouldn't even be feeding him but she couldn't bear to see anything starve to death.

She fed him as fast as he would eat, her eyes flipping repeatedly toward the tunnel mouth. What if Tolly decided to come back for something? Besides, the faster she fed the stranger, the less chance he had to talk.

When the food was gone, she gathered up her sack but he stopped her. 'Wait. Don't go.' His eyes held hers. 'Thanks for the food. My name is Brent.'

She started to say something. She felt an

impulse to talk. But she remembered the repeated warnings never to talk to a stranger should she meet one. This man, Brent he called himself, didn't seem vicious as she'd been led to believe all strangers who sneaked into Gunsight Canyon were supposed to be. In fact, he hardly seemed a stranger any more.

'I—I have to go,' she said softly.

'Untie me,' he said. 'I won't hurt you.'

She thought of the dire consequences if she turned the stranger loose and Joel or Tolly or anybody found out who did it. She shook her head.

'I can't. I—I'll bring more grub tomorrow.'

She picked up the candle and hurried away but his words, 'Thanks for the food,' followed her. She couldn't remember when anybody had ever thanked her for anything. It was a good sound. It put the stranger, Brent, in a world apart from the one in which she lived.

Virgie slipped out of the mine tunnel, checking the valley before venturing out into the open. No one was in sight. She hurried down into the trees, and then scurried along the creek toward home. If she was gone too long, she'd have trouble explaining her absence.

Emma did ask where she'd been, and she volunteered that she'd wanted to do some thinking and had gone off by herself. Emma didn't seem to consider that unusual and the matter was dropped. Joel and Zeke were still out searching for the intruder and Tolly hadn't come back since he left early this morning.

The day passed slowly. Virgie figured that either Joel and Zeke would find the stranger, or Tolly would make some foolish move and reveal where he'd hidden him. But evening came and the men returned. Because nothing had happened, Joel was as touchy as an aggravated snake.

'Lud says nobody went through the canyon mouth,' Joel told Emma, his face pulled down into a frustrated scowl. 'And Ike swears nobody got past him in the night. That stranger must still be in the canyon. We'll get him tomorrow.'

'What'll you give me if I help?' Tolly asked.

Joel turned his scowl on his youngest son. 'A good swift kick if you get in the way.'

'I'll bring him in if you'll promise to let me go out of the canyon like Zeke and Lud,' Tolly said.

'Huh!' Zeke exploded. 'I can just see you dragging in that stranger.'

Tolly ignored Zeke. 'How about it, Pa? Promise?'

'No!' Joel thundered, and Tolly recoiled, slinking off to the corner of the room.

Virgie watched Tolly, wondering if he was going to tell where Brent was. After Joel's roaring rebuke, she doubted if he would say any more. She saw that Tolly really did intend to blackmail Joel into letting him go outside the Canyon.

Ike Starry came in from the lean-to to gulp down his supper before going down to the mouth of the canyon, to relieve Lud for the night. He looked over the others, who would wait for their supper until Lud came in. His eyes fastened on Virgie. Her skin crawled like it did when she saw a snake coiled in her path. There was something about Starry, especially when he stared at her, that caused a hideous feeling of revulsion to encompass her.

As soon as supper was over and the dishes washed, she set the big bowl of cornmeal mush out to cool. They'd had cornmeal mush and milk for supper. It was Tolly's job to milk the cow that roamed the small pasture close to the house. Tomorrow morning Virgie and her mother would slice the stiffened mush and fry it. It was the men's favorite breakfast. But it took so long to fry that mush. They'd have to start breakfast a half hour earlier than usual.

In bed at last, Virgie found it impossible to sleep. Her thoughts kept going back to that stranger tied up in the mine. Even though Brent surely must have realized he was facing death, he still was able to thank her for feeding him. She had never known anyone quite like Brent, and she was sure she would not know him for long. If Tolly didn't kill him, Joel or Zeke would, when they found him.

She couldn't let it happen. If it was in her power, and she thought it was, she would free him as he had asked. If Tolly just didn't lose his temper and give away the place where he'd hidden the stranger before she could get to him.

Breakfast dragged on for hours, or so it seemed to Virgie. Then Lud had to go down to the canyon mouth, and Ike Starry came in for late breakfast. Virgie stayed out of the dining room while he ate and let her mother feed him. He didn't leer at Emma.

Then Starry went to his lean-to. The men were gone and the sheep were grazing. Virgie slipped some bread and meat, and a big slice of fried mush into the same sack she'd used yesterday and eased out of the house.

She didn't see Tolly today and she feared she would find him in his hideout. But when she got to the tree in front of the mine, she peeked inside the tunnel and saw it was dark. Tolly wasn't there or he'd have the candle burning. She lit the candle and hurried back to Brent.

'I'm glad to see you, Virgie,' Brent said as soon as he recognized her. 'I've got to get out of here. Tolly says he's going to turn me over to his pa today, and then he'll get to go outside the canyon.'

'He won't get out,' Virgie said. 'Pa won't ever let him out. Or me, either.' She started at him in the flickering light. 'Will you promise me something?'

Brent nodded. 'Anything, I reckon, if you'll

let me loose. I don't dare pull on this pole or the whole roof will cave in.'

She glanced at the ceiling and nodded in agreement. 'If you'll promise not to move till I'm gone, I'll untie you.'

'I promise,' Brent said quickly.

'You can eat this grub after I'm gone.'

Again Brent nodded.

Swiftly she untied the knots holding him to the pole. They were tighter than she expected them to be, but she got them loose. Then she turned and fled, thinking what would happen to her if anyone found out what she'd done.

CHAPTER EIGHT

Brent sat still and watched Virgie run out of the tunnel, stopping at the mouth only long enough to blow out the candle and set it on the rock. Left in the dark, Brent tested the ropes against his arms. When he moved, they fell to the ground. Virgie really had untied them.

It took a while for Brent's eyes to acquaint themselves with the dark again. Within a couple of minutes, he could make out the sack that she had left and he reached for it. The food was good. The slice of fried mush even had a lingering warmth to it.

He was just finishing the last of the food in the sack when he heard a noise at the mouth of the cave. He thought of trying to hide, but knew he couldn't. If that was Tolly, he'd know every nook in this mine far better than Brent did. All he knew was the area around this pole holding up the ceiling.

Grabbing the sack, he pushed it behind the pole then shifted into his original position, trying to shove the ends of the ropes back out of sight. Tolly wouldn't expect him to be free and maybe wouldn't notice that he was.

The candle flared at the end of the tunnel and then came wobbling toward Brent. In the flickering gleam of the candle, Tolliver walked, stiff-legged at Tolly's side as if anticipating an enemy with every step.

'Going to take you down to see pa,' Tolly announced. 'He won't believe I got you. I'll show him. Then he'll know I'm smarter than Zeke or Lud.'

Brent tensed. When Tolly started to untie him from the pole, he would discover that he was already loose. How would his feeble mind react to that?

Brent realized he'd have to be ready for anything. His eye was on the dog as much as Tolly. It would be the dog that he couldn't handle. He could surprise Tolly and overpower him in a minute, but not with that dog here.

Tolly moved closer to Brent then suddenly stopped, holding the candle down toward him.

'You're untied!' he exclaimed. 'Who let you loose?'

Brent brought his arms around in front of him. 'You don't tie knots as well as you thought,' he said.

Tolly dropped the candle and dived at Brent, apparently intent on pinning him to the pole while he pulled the ropes back in place. Brent leaned forward to meet the charge but he hadn't anticipated such a move by Tolly, and the force of Tolly's charge drove him back against the pole.

Brent heard the sharp crack before any of the falling dirt hit him. He slammed against Tolly, not in an effort to overpower him, but to get away from the falling ceiling. Rocks pelted him as he scrambled on hands and knees toward the entrance of the mine tunnel. Dust swirled up and choked him.

Brent continued to crawl forward, even after the rubble stopped. The dust was stifling, taking his breath, making him cough. He felt the wall at his back and he leaned against it, waiting for the air to clear. The candle had been snuffed out when the ceiling fell, and was most likely buried under the rubble.

Brent heard the rumbling growl of Tolliver before he saw him. Without the candle, all he could do was wait for the air to clear and his eyes to get used to the near darkness again. He had to anticipate Tolly's moves. But, Tolly had come in from outside just recently and, without the candle, his eyes would be more unaccustomed to the darkness than Brent's were.

The dust gradually settled and Brent could breathe freely again. His eyes slowly adjusted to the darkness. He saw the dog first. Tolliver had dodged back from the rubble as it fell from the ceiling, and apparently hadn't been hit by the rocks. Brent hadn't been that lucky. Now that he was momentarily safe from falling rocks, he realized that his legs and back had taken a pounding.

The dog was watching Brent, but he was inching toward the pile of rubble that stood where the pole had been. Brent's eyes tried to penetrate the darkness and the dust to see if Tolly was there. Tolly and the dog were inseparable.

Then he saw him. The upper half of Tolly's body was above the rubble but he was buried from the waist down. He seemed to be unconscious. The dog had moved over to stand protectively beside him.

It was Brent's chance to get out of the cave and away from Tolly. He had no idea how seriously Tolly was hurt. He might be dead; he wasn't moving. It was certain that Brent wasn't going to get close enough to find out if Tolly was alive or not. Tolliver was making sure of that.

Brent turned toward the mouth of the tunnel but then he stopped. He couldn't leave Tolly without knowing how he was. If he was dead, there would be nothing he could do. But if he was only hurt, he should try to get him out of the rubble and do what he could for him. Only Virgie knew about this hideout so far as he knew. He was sure that if Joel or Zeke knew about it, they already would have been here looking for Brent. There was no telling when Virgie might come back and find Tolly. Even if he was alive now, he could be dead before he was rescued.

But the moment Brent moved toward Tolly, Tolliver bared his teeth and raised the bristles on his neck. Brent knew better than to crowd his luck. Tolliver wasn't trying to attack him. He was just protecting Tolly. It was a standoff and Brent had no intention of breaking it.

For twenty minutes Brent waited, uncertain what to do. Again he reminded himself that he should be getting out of here, but couldn't leave without knowing whether he could help Tolly. He told himself over and over that he certainly didn't owe Tolly anything. After all, it was Tolly's fault that they were in this mine.

Then Tolly stirred and opened his eyes. Brent started toward him but stopped again when Tolliver growled and bared his teeth. Tolly blinked his eyes as he began to comprehend the situation. He tried to free himself but couldn't move anything but his arms and head.

'How did you do this to me?' he demanded finally.

'You did it to yourself,' Brent said. 'You

said that the roof would cave in if that pole was moved. You slammed into it.'

'How am I going to get out?'

'You're not unless you send that dog away so I can dig you out.'

Tolly was quickly regaining his senses. 'You'd dig me out?' he asked incredulously.

'Not with that dog ready to eat me alive,' Brent said.

'Tolliver, lie down!' Tolly said.

The dog took a step away, then turned to look at his master. Tolly repeated the order and the dog moved over against the wall and reluctantly lay down. Brent, now able to move forward, began clawing away the rubble, lifting off the biggest chunks of rocks. Tolly watched him, more in amazement than relief.

Before he got the last rocks off Tolly's legs, he discovered the candle, buried but unbroken. Then he got the last of the rubble away from Tolly, and the boy gingerly pulled himself free. Brent was surprised that he could use his legs and stand up.

'Why didn't you run?' Tolly asked finally. 'I was going to take you to Pa and he'd have killed you sure.'

'I couldn't leave you half buried in that rock pile,' Brent said.

'Why?' Tolly repeated. 'I would have left you.'

'Maybe we're different,' Brent said. 'Now you'd better get out of here.'

'Where are you going?'

'Where you won't find me again,' Brent said.

That seemed to satisfy Tolly. Picking up the candle, he went to the front of the tunnel and set it on the rock there. Then he and his dog disappeared outside.

Brent followed them to the front of the cave. He wanted to be sure that Tolly wasn't going to lie in wait for him, to recapture him again. There was no way to figure how a mind like Tolly's might work. Brent had to find Virgie as quickly as possible. He had come into the canyon on the afternoon of the thirteenth. This was the morning of the sixteenth. He'd spent two nights and most of two days in that mine. If he was to meet the deadline Zarada had given him, he had to get Virgie to Greeley by the twentieth. Only four more days. He'd better accomplish more in the next four days than he had in the last three.

Outside the mine, he stood in the shade of the tree until his eyes became accustomed to the sunlight. It seemed like a month since he'd seen the sun. He caught a glimpse of Tolly and his dog down along the creek. They were heading downstream toward the ranch. Apparently Tolly had no intention of trying to recapture Brent.

Brent moved out on the trail and hurried down into the trees. He crossed the creek and got into the aspens that had protected him the first afternoon he had arrived in the canyon. As he moved down the canyon, he passed the sheep, guarded by the dogs. He wondered if Virgie would come after the sheep this evening. Somehow he had to find her, convince her that he meant her no harm, and explain why he was here. He had judged that she was very intelligent but she'd had it drilled into her that strangers came here only to do her harm. He had to overcome that fear before he could explain the real situation. His first task, however, was to get her alone and make her listen to him. She'd had the advantage of being able to run away from him in the cave.

He came to a point even with the cabin and watched it for a half hour. But he saw no stir around the house. Virgie was surely there but she must be inside, likely on strict orders to stay there until the stranger was eliminated.

Brent moved on down the canyon, hoping to locate Joel and Zeke before they spotted him. If he was going to avoid them, he had to know where they were. He suddenly stopped when he was only half way to the mouth of the canyon. Lud, who watched the gap during the daylight hours, was coming up the canyon, prodding a big man at the end of his rifle barrel.

Brent didn't move until they passed him, no more than a hundred yards from his hiding place. He recognized Murdo Nanz, Jarron

Dix's right hand man. What was Nanz doing here? He wondered if the big gunman realized how fortunate he was that it had been Lud guarding the gap when he showed up. If it had been Starry or Joel or Zeke, he'd be a dead man now.

Brent reversed his direction, staying parallel with Lud and Nanz as they made their way to the cabin. Brent guessed that Joel was expected to be at the cabin now or Lud wouldn't be herding his prisoner that way.

As Lud reached the cabin and he and Nanz went inside, Brent crouched in the aspens across the creek from the cabin and waited. He half expected to hear gunshots and see Joel and his sons dragging Nanz's body out the door.

While he waited, he searched for some reason for Nanz being here. He must have been ordered here by Dix. But why? Had Dix heard somehow that a girl who might be Virgie Pool was here and had sent Nanz to kill her?

The door of the cabin opened again and Joel Kurtzman came out. Behind him came Murdo Nanz followed by Zeke and Lud. Brent watched in disbelief. The men seemed cautious but amiable. Brent wondered what Nanz had told them to win their confidence.

A few minutes later Starry joined the men outside the cabin, apparently awakened by the disturbance of Nanz's visit. Then Lud and Nanz started down the canyon again, this time walking together. Nanz was no longer a prisoner.

Brent wondered what could possibly have taken place to put Nanz in the good graces of the Kurtzmans. Joel, Zeke and Starry seemed to be involved in an animated conversation down close to the cabin and their voices rose as they began to argue. Brent couldn't understand what they were saying but if he somehow could move in a little closer, he might find out how Nanz fit into this picture. Brent had the feeling that Virgie's life hung in the balance.

Moving forward in the trees, he tried to get close enough to hear what was being said. Suddenly a dog began barking furiously at the corner of the cabin. Brent dropped down in a crouch. He had been sure all the dogs were out with the sheep. But at least one wasn't. The dog was looking across the creek almost directly at Brent's hiding place. Maybe he had scented Brent, or possibly had heard some sound Brent had made.

The three men suddenly turned their attention to the dog. Joel said something to Zeke, who turned and went back into the cabin. Brent knew he had gone after his rifle.

Brent weighed his chances. He didn't have any gun; Tolly had taken it when he captured him two days ago. He could run now or try to hide. He decided he had little chance to hide, especially since the dog had located him. If he waited another second to run, Zeke would come out while Brent was still within rifle range.

He leaped up and began running back into the trees. Joel's yell echoed over the canyon. But Brent disappeared into the dense thicket of trees before Zeke could get outside.

Brent wished that he had turned the other way this morning when he got out of that cave and gone over the wall by Gunsight Rock and just disappeared. Dix would have gotten Pool ranch, but Brent would still have his hide without holes in it. Now his chances of escaping Zeke and his rifle appeared pretty dim. At least, the Kurtzmans didn't have horses handy to use in running him down. In this canyon, they didn't ride much. Their saddle horses and the team they used to pull their buckboard were a quarter of a mile from the cabin, running loose in a pasture.

A rifle roared and a bullet spanged into a tree close to Brent. Zeke had seen him but he couldn't get a closer shot at him as long as he ran through the trees. Zeke was a short, heavy man. Brent doubted if he was a fast runner. Starry might be something else. But if Zeke hadn't brought a rifle for Starry, he doubted if he would hand over his to a fleeter man. Zeke would want to be in on the kill himself.

Brent turned down the canyon since the trees seemed to be thicker that way. He ran near the canyon wall to put as many trees between him and Zeke as possible. When another rifle shot came his way, he felt a touch of hope as he realized the rifleman was farther behind than when he had first shot.

Up ahead, Brent suddenly saw the rough front of a cabin. It looked pretty dilapidated but it offered a place to hole up if he could just get inside before Zeke and Starry saw where he went. Glancing back, he couldn't see any sign of his pursuers.

Judging from that last rifle shot, Zeke was losing ground fast. Brent doubted if Starry would try to get ahead of Zeke unless he had a rifle and Brent knew only one rifle had been fired at him so far. Brent might have time to get inside the cabin before they came in sight.

The door of the cabin was still on its leather hinges but it stood open. Brent dived inside and turned to look out through a glassless window. No one was in sight. He was sure he had made it. Looking around the cabin for a hiding place in case his pursuers investigated the cabin, he discovered that it was a one room affair. There wasn't space for any more than the one room, Brent realized. It was butted up against the canyon wall. An old stove sat against one wall with no pipe. A weathered tree stump that evidently had been used for a stool lay on the floor. A burlap sheet hung from the ceiling, covering the entire back wall.

There was no place for Brent to hide in here. His only hope was that Zeke and Starry and Joel, if he was along, wouldn't look in the cabin. They probably knew it was bare and wouldn't expect anybody to try to hide in it.

Through the window, Brent saw Zeke and Starry break into the open fifty yards away. They stopped, puffing, apparently discussing their next move. Zeke appeared to be ready to drop but Starry was still fresh. It was Zeke, however, who held the rifle. Starry had only a six-gun.

It was Starry who pointed to the cabin and Zeke nodded. Then they both began moving that way. Brent looked around frantically. He was unarmed. He knew what would happen when Zeke and Starry found him here. If he left the cabin, Zeke would pick him off as he would a deer. He was trapped.

CHAPTER NINE

Brent saw Starry pointing to the ground. Apparently he had located Brent's tracks leading to the cabin. Starry and Zeke began approaching cautiously, catching their breath. They had him trapped and they were sure of it.

Brent wheeled to look over the cabin again. There was nothing he could use as a weapon. His eye fell on the burlap curtain hanging from the ceiling against the back wall. Could he hide behind it? His body might make a bulge

95

wherever he stood and show them where to shoot to riddle him with bullets. Even that chance was better than standing out here in the open, just waiting to be shot.

Jerking up the corner of the burlap, he stepped behind it and worked his way out toward the middle. The burlap was almost against the rock wall. He knew he was pushing the burlap out of shape with his body.

Then suddenly his hand, reaching ahead along the wall, touched nothing. He moved a step farther and discovered there was a hole running back into the wall. It was barely big enough for him to stand in if he stooped. He realized that this might have been the mine of the man who had built the cabin. Maybe this had been the way he had made sure no one jumped his claim while he was asleep.

Brent moved back several feet into the tunnel and stopped, listening. For a while all was quiet, then he heard a thump as a man leaped through the door. Brent could imagine the man's consternation when he found no one in the cabin. Another set of boots thumped on the floor.

'You said you saw his tracks coming in here!' Zeke roared. 'He ain't here. Look for yourself.'

'I see he ain't,' Starry said. 'But his tracks came in here.'

'Maybe they came out, too,' Zeke said sarcastically. 'One look in this shack and any fool could see he couldn't hide here.'

'If you'd kept up with me or given me your rifle, I'd have been close enough to see that he didn't stop here,' Starry said indignantly. 'Let's get on with it. He must have headed for the gap, hoping to slip by Lud and Nanz.'

Boots thumped on the floor again and then all was quiet. Brent waited for five minutes before venturing out to the burlap sheet. He wondered why they hadn't brought along the dog. He would have sniffed him out. But, apparently the dog that had sounded the alarm hadn't been inclined to be a hunting dog today, and Zeke and Starry probably had been sure they could run down a man on foot who had shown no inclination to fight.

Brent slid along behind the burlap until he came out at the corner of the cabin. Before leaving the cabin, he decided he could use this place as his own hideout. Zeke apparently didn't know about the mine tunnel, so it was very likely none of the other Kurtzmans did, either. Brent might need a refuge like that sometime before he got Virgie out of this canyon.

Now that the Kurtzmans had actually seen him, they'd be more determined than ever to kill him. He'd have to watch Murdo Nanz, too. Jarron Dix had sent him for a purpose, most likely to kill Virgie. But there could be no doubt that Brent would also be fair game for him.

Leaving the cabin, Brent headed back up the canyon. Zeke and Starry had evidently gone on toward the mouth of the canyon. Virgie would be up at the house and she was the one he had to find.

That proved to be much easier than he had anticipated. Before he was halfway back to the house, he suddenly came face to face with Virgie as he dodged through the aspens. Both stopped in amazement. Brent realized that he had been pretty careless. That could have been Zeke or Joel just as well as Virgie who surprised him.

'I was watching for you,' Virgie explained. 'I saw you over there when Zeke and Ike took after you. I was hoping you'd get away.'

'I'm glad there's one person in the canyon who isn't trying to kill me. What's Nanz doing here?'

'I don't know,' Virgie said. 'Says he's dodging the sheriff and needs a job. Pa says he needs another man till he catches you, so he's giving Nanz a trial. Lud took him down to the gap to show him that job. Lud hates it.'

Brent realized suddenly that Virgie was actually talking to him. For the first time, her fear of him seemed to be fading. 'You've got to stay away from Nanz,' he said. 'I know him. I think he may be here to kill you.'

She gasped. 'Me? What for?'

'I'll tell you but it'll take a while.'

'You don't have time to tell stories now,'

Virgie interrupted. 'I came to warn you that this new man says you're a killer. Pa is more determined than ever to get you. He's offered twenty-five sheep to anybody who kills you.'

'I had a bigger price than that on my head when I came here,' Brent said. 'Ever hear of Jarron Dix?'

Virgie shook her head. 'Who is he?'

'He's a relation of yours,' Brent said. 'You'll soon be eighteen and when you are, you'll inherit a big ranch out on the plains that your father left you. But if you're dead, Jarron Dix gets it. He wants you dead and Murdo Nanz is his man. He's probably here to kill you.'

Brent could see that she was totally baffled. He hadn't done a very good job of explaining. He'd been too surprised at her sudden appearance to think of the best way to tell her.

'Pa don't own no ranch except this canyon,' Virgie said. 'And he wouldn't leave this to me, anyway.'

'You're not a Kurtzman,' Brent said patiently. 'Your name is Virginia Pool. Your real folks called you Virgie. They were killed and you were kidnaped by Joel Kurtzman.'

She shook her head. 'I'm Virgie Kurtzman,' she said positively. 'I've always been. You're trying to trick me.'

'I'm telling the truth,' Brent said. You've got to get out of this canyon and go to Greeley so you can claim your ranch.'

He could see that she didn't believe him. He

tried to think of some way to prove what he was saying. But he didn't get a chance.

Virgie gasped, and he suddenly became aware that something was wrong. He wheeled to face Murdo Nanz, who had a gun in his hand.

'Well, well,' Nanz said with relish. 'This is going to be an easier job than I figured.' His eyes swept Brent for a gun. 'Not even armed. Both pigeons in one cage.'

Brent started to back away. Nanz waved the gun barrel.

'Stay put,' he said. He moved closer. Slowly he slid his gun back in its holster. 'Don't want to rouse the neighborhood by using this. Won't be necessary anyway.'

Brent stared at Nanz. He was a gunman. He wouldn't put his gun away to fight with his fists unless he had a good reason. Perhaps he realized that a gunshot would be heard all over the canyon. Brent didn't doubt that Nanz could handle the situation with his fists, all right.

'Now!' Brent suddenly shouted and gave Virgie a shove. She reacted like a startled bird and dived into the trees.

Nanz lunged toward her, proving to Brent that it was Virgie he was really after. Brent dived toward Nanz, sticking out a leg that caught Nanz's foot. Brent was knocked down but Nanz tripped hard and landed against a tree.

Brent was on his feet instantly, his ankle throbbing from the blow it had taken when Nanz kicked it. But Nanz had banged his head against the tree trunk when he fell, and was slower getting to his feet. Brent lost no time, dodging into the trees and disappearing before Nanz had recovered enough to know in which direction he had gone.

Brent didn't go far but stopped where he could still see Nanz. He watched him as he rubbed his head and looked around. He could imagine Nanz's fury because he had been outsmarted. Brent wondered what he would do now. If he started after Virgie, he'd follow and try to stop him.

But Nanz, after kicking around disgustedly for a minute, turned and went back down the canyon toward the mouth. Brent, keeping in the trees, followed. He had to halt once and duck out of sight while Zeke and Ike Starry made their way back up the canyon on the other side of the creek. Nanz also kept out of their sight.

At the mouth of the canyon, Nanz went back to the rocks where Lud was watching. Brent couldn't get too close, but he could hear snatches of what the two said. He gathered from what he heard that Lud had been ordered by Joel to show Nanz how to guard the gap and that Nanz was to take a hitch at it after he became familiar with the job and realized its importance. Nanz had looked the canyon over now and was aware of the avenues a fugitive could take trying to slip past the guard and get out of the canyon. Brent realized that was what he supposedly had been doing when he ran into Virgie and him.

Brent remained in his hiding place until Lud handed over his rifle to Nanz and left, walking up the canyon. Brent assumed that Lud really must be tired of that daily job of guarding the gap to make him turn over the responsibility to Murdo Nanz when the Kurtzmans had known him only a couple of hours.

As soon as Lud was out of sight, Nanz lifted the rifle above his head and waved it back and forth. Brent thought that must be a signal to someone outside the canyon and he left his hiding spot and moved closer, sinking down in the rocks.

After a couple of minutes, Nanz signaled again. Then Brent heard someone moving over the water-washed rocks in the gap. The little stream that cut the valley in two ran out into the main canyon through the gap, fluctuating in size according to the melting snow on the peaks above it.

Brent frowned when he saw Jarron Dix move up to the rocks where Nanz waited. If there had been any question as to whether Dix had ordered Nanz to come to the canyon, it was gone now. Nanz's job had been to replace the guard at the gap and let Dix in. He had accomplished it without murder and probably in less time than even Dix could have expected.

'Good work,' Dix said when he reached the rocks. 'Where's the kid who was guarding the place?'

'Heading back to the house,' Nanz said, pride in his voice. 'I'm working for old man Kurtzman now and my job is guarding this gap.'

Dix whistled softly. 'How did you manage that?'

'Convinced him I was on the run, and needed a job and a place to hide out. Kurtzman needed another man to help run down Brent Clark so he hired me. Lud has been doing day duty here and he's so sick of it he can't eat. As soon as I told him I knew what he wanted done, he hightailed it back to the house.'

'Have you seen the girl?' Dix asked.

Nanz nodded. 'Yeah. Saw her and Brent Clark. I could've killed them both but I'd have had every Kurtzman in the valley on my head if I'd fired a shot. You said not to stir up anything till you got in.'

'If those two were dead, I wouldn't have cared if I hadn't gotten in. But if they're both here, we'll get them. Any chance that they'll come back here to relieve you soon?'

'I don't think so,' Nanz said. 'But they might check on me.'

'Let's get away from here where we won't be

interrupted and plan our moves. We should be through and out of the valley in an hour or two.'

Brent stayed down in the rocks as the two big men left the post and moved up the valley. When they were out of sight, Brent followed. He didn't have any idea what he would do, but he knew he had to stop them before they got to Virgie. It was clear enough that Dix's plan was to kill Virgie and him. Then there would be nothing standing in his way of taking over Pool ranch in just four days. Somehow his getting Pool didn't seem as important to Brent as it had a few days ago. What was important now was that Dix was intent on killing Virgie.

Brent moved through the trees carefully, knowing he could stumble onto the two of them if he wasn't careful. Even with all his care, he almost did just that. He heard a low voice just ahead an instant before he would have stepped around in sight of the pair.

Crouching down behind a couple of aspens that were growing close together, he peered between the trunks at the two men. They were halted, their backs to him. But they were unusually still. Suddenly they both whirled, each with his gun in his hand. Brent realized with a sinking heart that they had heard his approach.

He considered trying to run but he knew he wouldn't get ten feet. He was within fifteen feet of them and if he left the shelter of the aspens, they'd pick him off like a rabbit.

Dix nodded his head to the right and Nanz began circling that way, while Dix went to the left. Within seconds, Brent found himself sandwiched between the guns of the two men.

'This is one of them,' Dix said with satisfaction.

'Shall we beef him now?' Nanz asked eagerly.

'Don't get proddy,' Dix said. 'You said yourself that a shot now would bring all the Kurtzmans down on us. We've got to get that girl before they find out we're after her and hide her. She's more important than Brent.'

'Club him to death?' Nanz suggested.

Again Dix shook his head. 'You might botch that job. Take him to one of the mines, and when you get him back where a shot won't be heard in the valley, you take care of things. I'll go after the Pool girl. If the Kurtzmans heard a shot now, you can bet we'd never see her.'

Nanz nodded. 'Reckon you're right. I'll take care of Brent.' He hesitated. 'Maybe you'd like to take care of Brent yourself. I can find the girl again.'

Dix looked sharply at Nanz. 'I want them both dead. But it's the girl I want most. If the girl is pretty, you'd be just as apt to kiss her as kill her.'

Nanz grinned. 'Kissing her wouldn't be so bad. She's a looker. But if I have to beef Brent, there ought to be a bonus in it for me.'

Dix frowned. 'You're already getting extra wages for this job. But I'll make it worth your while to get rid of him.'

'How much?' Nanz insisted.

'We'll figure that out later,' Dix said irritably. 'We're losing time. What's the layout up ahead?'

'I've seen those buildings,' Nanz said eagerly. 'Maybe you'd better let me go after the girl, after all.'

'I'll get her,' Dix snapped. 'Tell me about those buildings.'

Nanz frowned. 'Good-sized log cabin, sheep barns and pens. All on the west side of the creek. Little cow pasture west of the house. Small barn at the corner of the pasture where they milk the cow. That's about it. Hard to slip up on the house without being seen, especially if they're watching.'

Dix said, 'I'll manage. You take care of Brent.'

He turned into the trees. Nanz prodded Brent toward the east wall of the canyon. Brent considered balking. Nanz would likely shoot him but he was going to die anyway, and a shot would alert the Kurtzmans to the presence of gunmen in the canyon. It might save Virgie. On the other hand, it might not save her, and if he was dead, he couldn't do anymore to help her. He'd better do as Nanz said now, and hope for a break later.

'Get moving,' Nanz said irritably. 'If you

think I won't put a bullet in your brisket right here, just try me. I could smother the sound by poking the muzzle in your clothes. That would sure be a messy way to die.'

Brent realized that Nanz was unusually provoked at having to get rid of him instead of going after Virgie. Evidently Nanz had a weakness for pretty girls and Virgie was as attractive as any girl he was likely to see. Dix had likely seen Nanz's desire and doubted if Nanz would kill Virgie if he found her. Dix, however, would not be blinded to his goal by her beauty.

Brent stumbled ahead of Nanz's gun, wondering if he would even reach one of the mines before Nanz got angry enough to kill him, in spite of Dix's warning.

CHAPTER TEN

Virgie had paused in her flight from Nanz only long enough to look back and see Nanz sprawled against a tree. She wondered what could've happened to him, but then she saw Brent slip away into the trees in the opposite direction and she smiled to herself. Somehow Brent had gotten both of them free of the big man.

She turned and ran again, keeping as quiet as possible. When Nanz got to his feet, he might take after her. She knew she couldn't outrun him but she could dodge around and hide. She knew this canyon well. Nanz couldn't know it; he had just arrived this morning.

After a quarter of a mile sprint, Virgie paused and listened. She couldn't hear any sound in the trees behind her. Nanz must've given up. Maybe he'd gone after Brent. Even that thought didn't worry her too much. She felt that Brent could take care of himself. He had certainly done it just a few minutes ago.

Then her mind turned to what Brent had told her. Brent wanted her to believe that she wasn't Emma Kurtzman's daughter. She didn't want to believe that. She had often wished that Joel Kurtzman wasn't her father. She was afraid of him. But if Brent was telling her the truth, then Zeke and Lud and Tolly weren't her brothers, either.

Thinking of Zeke, she suddenly felt a chill. If he wasn't her brother she could hardly feel safe around him any more. She hadn't given it a thought before, except to think that she didn't have much sisterly love for Zeke.

Lud was different. If she was to learn the truth about herself, she'd have to get it from Lud or Emma. Zeke would never tell her, even if he knew. She doubted if Emma would because she was afraid of what Joel would do to her if she did. And Tolly wouldn't know. She and Tolly had the same birthday and she had often wondered about the coincidence.

Tolly, except for his childlike mind, seemed almost as old as she was. Emma said he was one year younger, however, just to the day.

When she arrived home, she found Joel pacing the yard in front of the house, his rifle cradled in his arms.

'Where've you been?' he demanded the instant he saw her. He stopped his pacing and Virgie thought he might hit her. He often hit the boys, but he had never hit her, except for an occasional slap when he felt particularly put out by her.

'I haven't been far, Pa,' she said.

'Don't go anywhere!' he said sharply. 'That stranger's still here in the canyon and, until we get him, you're not to go out of this yard.'

'Yes, Pa,' she said and hurried on into the house. She didn't want to give Joel a chance to ask any more questions.

Emma wasn't much calmer than Joel. Her nervousness showed in the way she flitted from one household chore to another, often not finishing one before starting the other.

'Zeke ain't back yet?' Virgie asked.

Emma shook her head. 'Ike and Zeke went after that stranger. Ain't seen hide nor hair of either one since. No shots, either, except when they first started out. If they'd got him, I reckon they'd have come back crowing about it.'

For half an hour, Virgie worked around the house, avoiding conversation as much as possible for fear her absence would be brought up again. Then Lud came in and Joel lashed out at him for leaving the new man in charge of the gap by himself. Joel immediately sent Lud out to help Zeke and Ike look for the stranger.

Virgie watched him go and knew that he was only going to go far enough to get out of sight of Joel and then he'd stop. He wasn't a manhunter. She wanted to talk to Lud and she knew about where he'd be. But how would she get past Joel?

Joel had heard something down to the northeast in the trees along the creek and headed in that direction like an avenging angel. Virgie guessed it was Zeke and Ike coming back, but it gave her the chance to slip out and talk to Lud. If he wasn't where she expected him to be, she'd get back to the house before Joel did.

Lud was at the little clearing next to the cow pasture fence. There was a tree there that had blown over but hadn't died. Its trunk, parallel with the ground, made a perfect seat for Lud. Lud liked to read poetry when he could get a book and if the words weren't too difficult for him. He also wrote little poems. Virgie often wondered what he would have been like if he had been brought up in a town where schools were an essential part of life.

'Thought you'd be here,' Virgie said.

'Don't tell Pa I was out here,' Lud said

quickly, grabbing up a scrap of paper and a stub pencil, and shoving them in his pocket.

'I won't,' Virgie promised. 'I want to ask you something, Lud. Am I adopted?'

Lud scowled. 'Who put that idea in your head?'

'Doesn't make any difference,' Virgie said. 'I want to know. Am I?'

'Course not,' Lud grumbled. 'Ask Pa. Or Ma.'

'Pa won't tell me anything. And Ma might not.'

'You got no business asking me something that I don't know nothing about,' Lud snapped angrily.

Virgie knew she wasn't going to get anything more from Lud. He had said she wasn't adopted, but the way he'd said it left a doubt in her mind.

'Let me see your poem, Lud,' she said, moving up closer to him.

Lud hesitated while the anger drained from his face. Virgie was the only one he'd let see his poems. He pulled the paper from his pocket and handed it to her. She ran her eyes over it. The writing was almost illegible and the poem wasn't good, but she pretended that it was.

'This is good, Lud,' Virgie said. 'Someday your poems will be read by lots of people.'

'Aw, I don't want lots of people reading them,' Lud said, embarrassed. 'I just want to write them for myself. And you, if you like them.'

'What do you know about this man Pa hired today?' Virgie asked, handing the paper back to Lud.

'Nothing more than what he said. I don't like him, but I was sure glad to get someone to take that job of guarding the gap. That job is worse than herding sheep.'

'Didn't Pa send you out to look for somebody?'

Lud nodded and sighed. 'He wants me to find that stranger. But I don't want to find him. If I did, I'd be supposed to kill him. I ain't no killer, Virgie. You know that. Guess I could be if Pa drove me hard enough, but if I don't find that man, I won't have to shoot him.'

Zeke suddenly broke into the little clearing, his face dark with anger. 'Pa said you'd be out here somewhere. I figured this'd be where. You're supposed to be helping us hunt that stranger.'

Lud had come to his feet when Zeke appeared. He backed off, but he wasn't fast enough to avoid Zeke's fist, which knocked him flat.

'Pa says you'd better kill that stranger if you see him.'

Lud crawled to his feet, a wild light in his eye. He picked up his rifle. 'I'll kill him!' he screamed. 'And I'll kill you and everybody else too!'

112

'Don't talk like a fool,' Zeke yelled after Lud as he plunged into the trees and ran like a madman down the canyon.

Virgie wheeled and ran back toward the house while Zeke was still looking after Lud. She was as afraid of Zeke as Lud was, although he had never done more than slap her once. Emma had seen that and had given Zeke a lecture that not even his temperament could override.

Emma was in the house alone when Virgie came in. She didn't even ask where she'd been. Virgie decided this was as good a time as any to see if Emma would tell her any more than Lud had.

'Ma, am I adopted?' Virgie asked bluntly.

Emma's mouth dropped open, and she stared at Virgie. 'I've heard some crazy questions in my time but that one takes the cake.'

'That ain't no answer, Ma,' Virgie said.

'Reckon it ain't,' Emma agreed. 'No, Virgie, you're not adopted. I've been going—'

Joel stormed in, interrupting Emma. 'That stranger is harder to catch than a greased pig. He'll be striking pretty quick. He's only got four days left.

Virgie looked at Emma but she didn't say anything, so Virgie put in a question, even though she knew she risked rousing Joel's wrath.

'What's going to happen in four days?'

113

'None of your business,' Joel snapped. 'But you stay inside this house,' and wheeled out again, cradling his rifle in his right arm, heading toward the creek to keep a watch for the stranger.

Virgie turned on Emma. 'Ma, what'd he mean by four days?'

Emma shook her head. 'If Pa don't want you to know, then I'm not going to tell you.'

'I don't have to stay cooped up here in the house do I?'

'You sure better not get too far away,' Emma said. 'I'll be glad when this all settles down and we can get back to living like we did.'

Virgie could agree with that except for thoughts of the stranger, Brent. He had brought a new dimension to her life and there was a vague promise in his presence that she hadn't quite grasped. He wanted her to leave the canyon. She knew she couldn't do that, but the thought did intrigue her. She had wanted to leave so often. What would she find out there? Surely not the terrible things Joel had led her to believe were out there. If Brent took her out, it might just be as wonderful as her dreams had envisioned.

Virgie wondered where Brent was now. With so many men looking for him, it was a wonder that he was still alive. Her father and brothers and now Nanz were all out to get him. Nanz also seemed determined to kill her, too, and that she did not understand at all.

Virgie slipped outside and went to the sheep shed. She wondered about getting very far from the house. There was a little nook not far from the clearing where Lud liked to go and write his poetry that she enjoyed more than any spot in the canyon unless it was the base of Gunsight Rock which gave her such an awesome view of the entire canyon.

It wasn't far and she decided to go up there and try to reason out some of the puzzles racing through her mind. She walked quickly through the trees to the little nook. It was hardly big enough to be called a clearing, but the trees offered shade and almost a wall against the problems of the canyon.

She had barely reached the place when she heard a tree branch snap beyond the clearing, sounding like sacrilege to the peace she had always found here. She hesitated, like a bird ready to take flight. Ordinarily a sound in the trees did not disturb her. But after what had been going on in the canyon the last two or three days, every sound could mean potential danger.

Then she saw a man coming through the trees, trying to be quiet but not succeeding at all. They saw each other at about the same time. At, first glance, she thought it was Nanz, but then she saw that it wasn't. He was almost as big as Nanz. How had all these strange men gotten into the canyon that her father had said was out of reach of the outside world?

The man began running toward her. She whirled and raced back toward the house. The man was big enough to run fast but he couldn't keep up with her. She knew every step of the way back to the house and how to dodge every tree and shrub in the path. Like a deer, she sped along, jumping over little bushes and ducking around trees.

Her heart almost stopped when she heard a rifle shot that splintered the bark of an aspen not far from her head. The man was shooting at her. The thought that somebody was actually trying to kill her seemed to put wings on her feet. She darted toward the house, ducking behind the sheep shed when she left the trees. She glanced back once but she couldn't even see the man now.

She saw Joel running up from the creek, his rifle held in both hands. She guessed it was cocked ready to fire. She left the sheep shed and ran on to the house. Emma was waiting for her and Joel came in, standing just inside the door, looking out, rifle ready.

'Who fired that shot?' Joel demanded.

'I don't know,' Virgie panted. 'I never saw the man before.'

'Did he shoot at you?' Emma asked.

Virgie nodded. 'He was a big man, about the size of Nanz but it wasn't him.'

'He probably looked bigger because you were scared,' Emma said.

Joel growled an oath. 'Dix,' he said. 'How'd he get in here?'

'Who's Dix?' Virgie asked. Brent had talked about Dix, saying Nanz was his man and warning her to stay away from Nanz. If Brent was right, then it followed that Dix would also be dangerous to her if he was here. It was beginning to look like Brent was right. If he was right about that, he was probably right about everything he had told her.

'Dix is a bad man,' Emma said. 'You must stay away from him.'

'Why'd he shoot at me?'

Joel didn't even look around or say anything, as if he hadn't heard. Emma had no answer.

'Dix has a grudge against Pa,' she said gently. 'He'd shoot at anybody that's in Pa's family.'

The answer didn't entirely satisfy Virgie, but she knew that was all the explanation she was going to get. Joel wouldn't have given her that much. There was no doubt about the fear in Emma. Joel even showed more uneasiness than she had ever seen before. Here in this valley where he was absolute king, she'd never seen him show the least hesitation about what to do, and he'd been completely ruthless in carrying out his decisions. Now that dominating confidence was gone.

Joel moved quickly between the two windows of the main cabin, checking for the gunman, then came back to the door. As the minutes dragged by, he made this circle more often.

Suddenly, while Joel was checking the window in the back of the house, Virgie caught a glimpse of movement near the sheep shed. She stepped quickly over where she could see out the door. The man who had shot at her was making a weaving dash toward the house.

'Pa!' she screamed. 'He's coming.'

Joel wheeled toward the front door, running across the floor as fast as he could. It was because he was moving so fast that he wasn't ready to use the rifle when the big man suddenly erupted into the doorway. He had a rifle and it was pointed directly at Joel's middle.

'Drop the rifle, Kurtzman!' the man said.

Joel stopped four feet from the door as if he'd run into a stone wall. For an instant, his face showed his inclination to take a chance that he could swing up the rifle and shoot first. But the bore of the big man's rifle was staring him convincingly in the face. Slowly, he loosened his fingers and the rifle clumped to the floor.

'What do you want, Dix?' he grumbled.

'Reckon you know what I want,' Dix said. He looked quickly over the house. 'You two just stay put without any quick moves,' he told Emma and Virgie. Then he turned his attention back to Joel. 'Where're your boys?'

'They ain't here,' Joel said.

'I can see that,' Dix said. 'I want to know where they are.'

'They'll be after your hide mighty quick, I can tell you that,' Joel said.

'They won't crowd me too close,' Dix said. 'I'll have Virgie with me.'

'No!' Emma said. 'You're not taking her.'

Dix turned blazing eyes on Emma. 'Who's going to stop me?'

Emma stood with clenched fists. As soon as Dix turned his attention back to Joel, she lunged at Dix. Dix barely looked at Emma. He swung the rifle barrel, catching Emma on the side of the head as she charged. Before Joel could take advantage of the diversion, the rifle barrel was back in his face.

Dix's face turned dark as a cloud. 'I won't slug the next one that moves,' he snapped. 'I don't care if I have to kill everyone here. That would suit me just fine. Want to try your luck, Kurtzman?'

Joel was breathing hard, like a man who had just run a half mile. 'I don't doubt that you'd like to kill us all. I promise you—you won't get away with it. My boys—'

'Your boys can't do a thing. They're not here, and by the time they get here, it'll be too late.'

Virgie dropped on her knees in spite of Dix's warning not to move. She felt Emma's pulse. It was strong and steady. She was just knocked out. Virgie knew that Dix intended to kill her. She didn't know whether it would be here, or somewhere out in the canyon. If Joel crowded him now, he'd kill them both right here. Emma might be spared since she was already unconscious.

'Come on,' Dix said sharply, motioning for Virgie to stand up. 'We're leaving.' He glared at Joel. 'If you want to try to stop me, that's fine. I wouldn't mind killing you.'

Joel scowled, but he didn't move. Virgie got to her feet and moved slowly toward the door. Dix backed out the door, keeping his rifle on Joel. Virgie came out and Dix backed away to the sheep shed. He kept Virgie between him and the house as he backed into the trees beyond the shed.

Virgie could hear Joel roaring back at the cabin and then she heard a faint reply from Zeke somewhere along the creek. Joel and Zeke and Lud would be on Dix's trail in a few minutes. But she knew that wasn't going to do her any good. Dix might kill her now, and then try to outrun the pursuit in getting out of the canyon. However, he was more likely to use her as a shield to protect him from the Kurtzmans until he got out. Then he'd kill her.

She had the feeling that Dix would shoot her right now except that would give away his exact location and bring retaliation from the Kurtzmans before he got out of the canyon.

Virgie had never been so scared in her life.

CHAPTER ELEVEN

Brent was pushed along the east wall of the canyon, keeping back far enough in the trees that anyone with a view of the foot of the canyon wall wouldn't see them. Nanz seemed to have an idea where he was going. Brent didn't.

Nanz kept looking back and checking the surrounding area. He was aware that there were Kurtzmans out looking for Brent and they might shoot him, too, if they discovered he had left his post at the gap.

A mine shaft burrowing straight into the canyon wall appeared ahead to the left. Nanz motioned that way with his gun, then centered it again on Brent's back.

'That ought to be a nice quiet place.'

'You don't think Dix is going to give you that bonus, do you?' Brent asked.

'I figure he will,' Nanz said. 'He'd better.'

'Or what will you do?' Brent prodded.

He shot a glance back at Nanz. Nanz was frowning. Brent's suggestion had gotten through to him. Like Dix, he was big enough he could usually get whatever terms he demanded. But Dix was about as big as Nanz and he was also good with a gun. No gunman wanted to go up against an equal if he could avoid it. Nanz was probably puzzling right now over a way to prevent that in case Dix reneged on his promise.

'He'll pay up,' Nanz said stubbornly.

'I wouldn't plan on it if I were in your boots,' Brent said.

They reached the mouth of the mine and moved inside. There Nanz halted Brent while he stood in the mouth of the tunnel and looked out, dividing his attention between the canyon and Brent.

Satisfied that no one had seen them, Nanz prodded Brent with his gun toward the mine.

Brent moved slowly, knowing that as soon as Nanz considered it safe to fire his gun, he'd be dead. The revolver wouldn't make as much noise as a rifle, but it still would echo over this canyon. Those steep walls on three sides threw back every sound made within their confines.

'Hold it,' Nanz said.

It already was getting gloomy, and Nanz was likely having trouble seeing every move Brent was making. Brent weighed his chances. They weren't good enough yet. Nanz would riddle him with bullets if he tried to get away now.

'Just don't try anything fancy,' Nanz warned. 'I can shoot you twice before you touch me.' He backed off a few more feet and suddenly a match flared in his hand.

By the light from the match, Nanz located a stick of wood that had splintered off the shoring on the tunnel. He picked it up and held the match to the small end of it. The match spluttered and went out but Nanz lighted another one, managing to keep the gun pointed in the general direction of Brent all the time.

The stick finally caught, giving off a soft glow that grew as the dry wood began to burn. A whiff of pine smoke carried to Brent.

'Now move ahead,' Nanz ordered.

Brent walked slowly. As they got deeper into the mine, he expected a bullet in the back any instant. He considered every dark nook on either side, wondering if he could dive into the dark somewhere and escape Nanz's bullets.

Then suddenly Nanz called him to a halt. Brent had seen the dark side tunnel to his right and had tried to inch that way to give himself a better chance of reaching its dark recesses before Nanz could fire. Now he was halted only three feet from this spot he had marked to make his desperation lunge.

'Turn down this side tunnel,' Nanz demanded.

Slowly Brent obeyed. He knew that once they were in the side tunnel, Nanz would probably shoot him. The sound of a shot would not carry out of a side tunnel like it would here, in the main shaft.

Just inside the side tunnel, Nanz called another halt. The shoring on this tunnel had collapsed back a ways, and wood was lying around everywhere. It seemed to give Nanz an idea.

'So you think I can't make Jarron pay me for handling this job, do you?' he said, revealing that Brent had really stirred up doubts with his suggestion that Dix wouldn't pay him.

'Why should he?' Brent said. 'You'll have the work done, and you can't undo it.'

'That's where I'm thinking faster than you are. And faster than Jarron, too. I'm going to lock you up in this shaft. Then if Jarron won't pay me, I'll threaten to turn you loose.'

Brent was surprised at that line of thinking. But he realized that it was a break for him. He likely would be bottled up here in the mine and might die here if something happened to Nanz. But the only other alternative was death right now.

As Nanz forced Brent up against the wall, he dug out a big kerchief, and used it to bind Brent's hands behind his back. Nanz then pushed Brent farther into the side tunnel, until he was in the rubble beyond the boards that had caved in from the ceiling of the tunnel.

Nanz carried some loose boards back to the mouth of the tunnel and fitted them across the framework around the tunnel mouth. Using the nails already in the boards and another heavy stick as a hammer, he drove the nails into the frame, making it almost air tight. All Brent could do was watch helplessly. The only way out was past Nanz, and he kept his gun within easy reach.

With each board that went up, it grew darker where Brent was. He looked around, trying to familiarize himself with his surroundings so he'd remember when he could no longer see. Nanz kept the torch on his side of the barrier.

Brent was already twisting his wrists, trying to loosen the kerchief that bound his hands. He thought the knot was giving a little, but he couldn't tell until he got a chance to put the pressure on it. He couldn't do that until Nanz could no longer see him.

That time came soon enough. When the last board had been nailed in place and tested by Nanz, it was pitch dark where Brent was. Brent heard Nanz shuffling around when he called to him.

'Ain't no use of you tearing around in there. You couldn't break through those boards even if your hands were free. And nobody is going to hear you if you yell.'

Brent didn't answer. Nanz was right. Nobody in this canyon would help him except Virgie and she would never come to this mine. In fact, Brent doubted if anybody had been in this mine since it had been abandoned many years ago.

He listened carefully but couldn't be sure just when Nanz did leave. First he had to get his hands free. By prying his wrists apart, he tightened the knot but loosened the cloth itself. Twisting until his arms ached, he finally got his hands free. He stuffed the kerchief into his pocket.

He felt his way to the end of the tunnel and tested the boards that held him prisoner. Here he was disappointed. Those nails were holding the boards so tight, it was as if a carpenter had used new nails and new lumber. He couldn't even make one of the boards squeal.

Sweating from his efforts to pry the boards loose, he backed off and felt around for a big rock in the rubble and sat down. His thoughts were more of Virgie than of himself. What would happen to her? Dix wanted her dead because of her inheritance. A flimsy excuse for murdering someone, especially a pretty girl like Virgie.

Funny, Brent thought, that he'd be thinking of Virgie as a pretty girl instead of just the girl he'd come here to steal out of the canyon, either by coaxing or kidnapping, to take to Greeley. Now, he realized, he wasn't as interested in getting her to Greeley on the appointed day as he was in seeing that no harm came to her.

But what could he do now? There was just no way that he could get out of this mine shaft. Nanz had done an exceptionally good job nailing up those boards. And there was certainly no way out of this shaft except past those boards.

He got up, found a piece of timber, and pounded on the boards. Again he couldn't even make a nail squeal. Finally, exhausted, he gave up and felt around for a smooth place where he could lie down. He needed to think and he needed to rest. At least, the floor here was bone dry. It was comfortably cool, too. He had just started to concentrate on his problem when he dropped off to sleep.

He had no idea what time it was when he woke up. It had been about evening when Nanz had brought him in to the mine. He wondered if it was morning or the middle of the night. There was no difference in light here in this tunnel. If it was morning, he had only three days to get Virgie to Greeley. But that didn't seem so important now. He might have only a few hours to keep her alive. Or he could be too late for that already.

He felt his way to the boards blocking the entrance to the tunnel. It was then that he realized what had awakened him. On the other side of the boards something was sniffing and a deep growl rumbled at him.

Instinctively, he backed off although the boards that kept him from escaping were also keeping that animal from getting to him. The growl came again, followed by some hard clawing. Whatever it was, it was trying desperately hard to get to him. From the growl, he decided it was a wolf or a dog. Tolly's dog, Tolliver! That was why that growl sounded so familiar. That dog would tear him to shreds if he got through that barrier.

Brent backed off where his scent wouldn't carry so well to the dog. Maybe he'd give up and go away. But the dog kept clawing. He'd tunnel under the boards in time.

Then he seemed to grow more excited, whining and clawing even harder. Brent couldn't understand his craze to get inside the tunnel. Then he heard a voice encouraging the dog.

'Sic 'em, Tolliver. Whatever is in there, he's all yours.'

Brent leaped back to the barrier. 'Tolly?' he called. 'Tolly?'

'Hold it, Tolliver,' the boy shouted. The dog stopped digging. 'Is that you in there, Brent?'

'It's me,' Brent shouted. 'Nanz nailed me in here and I can't get out.'

'I saw a bar back there,' Tolly said. 'Wait. I'll get it.'

Foolish advice, Brent thought. What else could he do but wait? He was sure now that Tolly would get him out. This would return the favor he thought he owed Brent for getting him out of the rubble in that other mine.

After a short time, Brent heard footsteps outside then something jammed against the boards. In a second, a nail in one of the boards began squealing as a pry from the other side loosened it.

The board came loose at one end and the light, dim as it was this far back from the main entrance, streamed in. Brent thought it equaled any sunrise he had ever seen. Tolly pried the other end of the board off, then attacked another one. In three minutes, he had enough boards off so that Brent could crawl out.

'What did Nanz lock you in there for?' Tolly asked.

'He was told to kill me. I figured I was lucky to get locked up instead of killed.' Brent eyed the dog who stood with bristles up, glaring at him.

'Tolliver is sorry you're not a rabbit,' Tolly said. 'He's our friend, Tolliver,' he said to the dog.

Watching the dog, Brent was sure that he didn't believe the boy. 'How did you happen to find me back here?'

'Tolliver found you,' Tolly said. 'Pa got mad at Tolliver last night and wouldn't let me feed him so I took him hunting this morning. He got on the trail of something a little way from this mine and followed it right in here. Must have been your trail. When I got here, he was trying to get through those boards.'

'Where is Virgie now?' Brent asked.

'I don't know,' Tolly said. 'After Pa got mad last night, me and Tolliver went out to my cave for the night.'

'Have you seen a man named Dix? He's almost as big as Murdo Nanz.'

Tolly shook his head. 'I got to find something for Tolliver to eat.' He turned and headed out of the mine at a trot. The dog growled once at Brent then, wheeling and passing Tolly, led the way out into the morning light.

Brent moved more slowly out into the light. The sun was shining brightly on the west side of the canyon but the east side was still in shadow. His stomach reminded him that he hadn't had anything to eat since Virgie had fed him yesterday morning.

He got his bearings and headed up the canyon. The mine where he had cached the food he'd brought from Zarada's was almost opposite the Kurtzman cabin. After he had something to eat, he'd consider his next move. Only three days now before he'd have to have Virgie at Greeley unless he wanted Dix to get Pool ranch. There were few things he wanted less than that.

Still unarmed, Brent made his way through the trees to the mine. He found his sack of grub untouched and filled up on meat and bread. In the cool mine interior, the meat seemed to have kept all right. He wished he had a gun. He hadn't had one since Tolly took his three days ago.

With his food running low and no gun, he had to get out of the canyon soon. He left the mine and circled around, hoping to come up close to the Kurtzman cabin without being seen. Virgie would surely be there. He wondered if she'd thought about what he'd told her. Maybe she would be ready now to go out of the canyon with him.

Below the cabin, he moved to the creek to cross but suddenly stopped dead in his tracks as he heard voices ahead. Two men were talking in low tones, and it wasn't likely to be any of the Kurtzmans. Unless they were stalking some intruder, they'd never speak softly.

Brent moved ahead cautiously until he saw two big men huddled close together in a thicket. Nanz and Dix. Even though they were keeping their voices down, there was no mistaking the fury in Dix's voice.

'I heard the Kurtzmans coming north of the house and I swung west. Then this little guy popped up with a gun right in my face and took the girl away from me.'

'Lud,' Nanz said. 'He don't even look like a Kurtzman. Where did he take her?'

'Back to the house, I suppose. I should've killed her when I had the chance. But as we've already realized, a shot then would've attracted the Kurtzman clan like honey draws a bear. At least, we got rid of Brent Clark.'

Nanz didn't say anything for a moment. 'How about that bonus?' he asked finally. 'I figure a little piece of Pool ranch would be a fair price.'

Dix swore viciously. 'You're figuring wrong. I'm not slicing up Pool with nobody. But since you got rid of Brent and if you'll help me get

131

Virgie, I'll put a thousand dollars in your pocket. Figure out how long it would take you to earn that much at regular wages.'

Nanz nodded, but Brent could see the scowl on his face. Nanz obviously doubted if Dix would honor that promise. Still, the two of them began making their plans to get Virgie. If they couldn't capture her outside the house, they'd wait till the men were off looking for the intruders in their canyon, then they'd storm the house.

'Wouldn't be more than one man there likely,' Dix said. 'We can handle one.'

Brent knew their plan might work. He had to get to Virgie first.

CHAPTER TWELVE

Brent eased back from the spot where he'd been eavesdropping on Dix and Nanz. At least, the two wouldn't be looking for him. Nanz thought he had him penned up where he'd starve to death; Dix obviously thought he was already dead. But they were expecting the Kurtzmans and they'd shoot to kill if they discovered anybody near them.

Brent hurried on toward the Kurtzman cabin. He had to get Virgie away from there before Dix and Nanz did. If they got Virgie in their possession again, they'd kill her before

132

there was a chance of anything happening to rob them of the opportunity.

The sun was hitting the cabin by the time Brent got close enough to see what was going on. Joel and Zeke, armed with rifles and six-guns, were just leaving the cabin. It took no imagination to guess what they were going to hunt for. They left both Lud and Ike Starry behind. Starry seemed to be assigned to the back of the cabin and Lud to the front.

With two guards at the house, Brent knew he had no chance of getting Virgie out. If only he had a gun! Zarada had said this was gun country. He was right, and Brent, without a gun, felt like a rabbit in the middle of a wolf pack.

He was fairly certain that Dix and Murdo Nanz wouldn't try to storm the cabin with both Lud and Starry there. Brent realized he could get out of the canyon easily now if he only had Virgie. No one was guarding the gap. Apparently Joel felt that all the men he had been trying to keep out of the canyon were already here.

Brent backed away from his vantage point and considered his next move. Virgie was as safe now as she could be with Nanz and Dix on the loose. There wasn't a thing he could do here. He couldn't get to her, either.

He headed back to the cave where he'd left his sack of grub. Getting it, he moved down the canyon to the cabin that stood in front of the mine tunnel. If he was going to use this for his refuge if pursuit got too close, he should have his food supply here, too.

Inside the cabin he went behind the burlap curtain and took his sack of grub back into the mine. Then he came out into the cabin and considered his next move. Somehow he had to get a gun. He had absolutely no chance of getting Virgie out of the canyon if he didn't have a gun.

He wondered if the previous occupant of this cabin had left anything that he could use for a weapon. There was a pile of gunny sacks in the corner of the room but when Brent examined them, he found nothing in or under them.

Going outside, he looked around the cabin. There seemed to be nothing more lethal than a stick of wood. Then on the north side of the cabin, close to the canyon wall, he found a couple of big bear traps hanging on nails.

He took them off their nails and carried them inside, not sure what he could do with them. They looked formidable. There must be some way he could use them for defense against surprise, at least.

First, he tried to set the traps. The biggest trap had springs too strong for him to press down. But the other trap, just a bit smaller, was a little easier to handle. By standing on the springs, he could press them down a little way, but not enough to flip the catch over the jaw and hook it under the plate.

Jumping on the springs brought them down far enough to let the jaws spread. But the first two times he jumped on the springs, the trap rolled, throwing Brent halfway across the room.

Then he set himself, made his jump, and maintained his balance and the springs stayed down. The big, toothed jaws of the trap flopped open. Carefully, he leaned over and flipped the catch across the jaw. With equal care, he reached a finger of the other hand under the opposite jaw and lifted the tongue of the trap. Inching the catch into the slot under the tongue of the trap, he held it while he eased the weight on one foot. The jaw of the trap came up against the catch and that held it in the slot under the tongue. Gingerly, he stepped off the springs of the trap. The trap was set and, considering how hard it was to do, he decided to leave it set until he could figure out where to put it outside so it would catch anyone trying to sneak up on him in the cabin.

Setting up the stump that had obviously been used for a chair, he carefully lifted the trap and put it on the stump. He knew that he could move the trap without springing it. He started outside to look for the right place to set it, where it would be most apt to catch an intruder.

He stopped just short of the cabin door as he heard a sound out in the trees not far from the cabin. Someone or some animal was out there. It was almost sure to be a man. The Kurtzmans had eliminated most of the bigger animals in the canyon that might kill sheep.

Stepping back into the cabin, his first thought was to get into the tunnel where they couldn't find him. But the trap stared him in the face. Anyone coming into the cabin and seeing that set trap would know someone was here. His hideout would no longer be a secret.

Looking frantically around the room, his eyes fell on the pile of gunny sacks. Grabbing one of them, he tossed it over the trap. If someone looked in, he might not examine that stump with a sack tossed over it. It looked innocent enough.

He wheeled toward the burlap curtain that hung over the back wall of the cabin. But just as he reached the corner of the curtain, a thump on the doorsill stopped him.

'Got you at last,' the man said as Brent wheeled.

Joel Kurtzman was in the doorway, his rifle aimed directly at Brent. Joel's eyes swept over Brent. His finger eased on the trigger as he saw that Brent was unarmed.

'No gun,' Joel said, panting, his voice lowering in satisfaction. 'This is real nice. Just like you were expecting me.'

'I was expecting Jarron Dix,' Brent said.

Joel's eyes lighted up. 'What do you know about Dix?'

Brent hesitated. 'Probably not as much as you do,' he said.

It was obvious that Joel was in no hurry now to shoot him. He wanted more information about Jarron Dix and he thought Brent could tell him. Brent didn't know much about him, but he wasn't going to tell Joel even that little bit. Holding back that information could be the only thing that would postpone his death, even for a few minutes.

'If you know he's here, you probably know how many men he has with him,' Joel snapped. 'So you'd better tell me.'

'Why should I?'

Joel brandished the rifle. 'If you don't, you'll get the business end of this.'

Brent wished he had made it into the tunnel behind the burlap curtain. 'If I do tell you, I'll still get the same thing.'

'That's for me to decide,' Joel said. 'You'll sure get it if you don't talk.'

Joel was still puffing, apparently from his run to the cabin door. He must have seen something that told him someone was in the cabin and he had given his best effort to surprise the occupant. His eyes dropped to the sack-covered stump.

Brent didn't miss the move. 'If you'll tell me exactly what you want to know, I'll tell you what I can,' he said, all defiance fading from his voice.

Joel nodded in satisfaction. He had things

completely under control now and he was tired. His eyes wandered to the stump again. Stepping over, he dropped down without brushing the sack aside.

The second he touched the trap, he realized something was wrong but it was too late. Joel was not a tall man but he weighed over two hundred pounds. Those pounds held the trap open even after the tongue had been pushed down and the catch released. The instant the weight came off those jaws, however, they would spring shut, their jagged teeth grabbing anything within, their reach.

'What—is—that?' he demanded, barely hissing the words.

'Just what you think it is,' Brent said. 'A bear trap. It's got very sharp, jagged jaws as you can probably feel. If you make a move, it'll take a big chunk out of your backside.'

'You set it deliberately,' Joel hissed.

I didn't invite you in,' Brent said. 'I wasn't even expecting company.'

'I'll kill you for this and enjoy every second.'

'If you fire that rifle, the jolt may move you enough to spring that trap,' Brent said. 'Besides, if you shoot me, who's going to get you off that trap without it taking half your back end with it?'

Joel's face turned red, then a sickly green. 'You'd better get me off this trap,' he said, still trying to sound threatening.

Brent grinned. 'You look too quiet and

138

peaceful for me to disturb you. You can drop that rifle. Or if you're afraid to move even that much, I'll just step over and get it.'

'I'll kill you,' Joel blustered.

'I doubt it. You don't have nerve enough to get up and let that trap take its bite out of you. And you don't want to sit there the rest of your life.'

Joel showed no signs of letting the rifle fall. Brent moved slowly around to a point where the rifle was no longer pointed at him. Then he stepped in close to Joel. Only Joel's eyes, filled with hate and fear, followed him. Reaching out, Brent grasped the rifle and lifted it gently from Joel's hand. Then he took the gun from his holster. Joel sat still, convinced that even a slight move might be enough to spring that trap. Brent could almost see him sitting as hard as he could, pushing all his weight down to hold those jaws open.

'Where is Virgie?' he asked.

'What's it to you?' Joel asked softly.

'I know Dix is here to kill her. I don't want to see her die.'

'Why do you care?'

Joel was stalling. Brent sensed it. Evidently Zeke was out there somewhere waiting for Joel to see what was in the cabin. Joel and Zeke had been together when Brent had seen them earlier this morning down by the Kurtzman cabin.

Brent moved to the wall next to the door

139

and peeked out, the rifle in his hand ready for use. Nothing moved out there.

'Either you tell me were she is or I nudge you with this rifle. All it'll take is a little push.'

Joel's face turned a shade greener. 'She's at the house. Lud and Starry are guarding the house. You can't get to her.'

'I'm more worried about Dix getting to her.' He looked out the door again. 'Who's out there waiting for you?'

'Nobody,' Joel said quickly.

'You had Zeke with you this morning, I reckon he's out there now. Want to call him in?'

'Ain't nobody with me,' Joel insisted, his voice rising a little.

'Then you won't mind yelling for whoever is there to come on in.'

'Ain't nobody there, I said.'

'If there isn't, then your yelling won't disturb anybody. Go ahead.' Still Joel hesitated. Brent aimed the rifle at Joel's foot. 'A bullet in the foot doesn't hurt as bad as one in the eye. But it will make you jump. Then that trap'll make you forget all about the bullet in your foot.'

Joel scowled, breathing hard. Finally, he yelled with only half his usual volume. 'Come on in, Zeke. I got him.'

Brent waited behind the half open door. From there he could see every move Joel made. Through the crack between the hinges, he could also see Zeke coming slowly from the trees. He was suspicious.

'You even bat an eye and I'll blast you in the foot,' Brent warned softly.

Everything was quiet as Zeke came closer. He saw his father sitting on the stump and apparently decided that he did have things under control. So he stepped boldly into the cabin.

Brent jabbed the rifle muzzle into his back. 'Drop your rifle and unbuckle that gun belt.'

Zeke caught his breath. 'You said you had him,' he hissed at Joel.

'He did,' Brent said. 'He had me right behind the door waiting for you.'

'I'm sitting on a bear trap,' Joel said.

'A bear trap!' Zeke exclaimed incredulously. 'How'd you get in that?'

Brent grinned. 'A bear doesn't ask how he got into a trap. The only thing he's interested in is getting out.'

'I'll get him out,' Zeke said, starting toward Joel.

'Not now!' Brent said sharply. 'Shuck your gun belt and rifle. Then we'll talk.'

Growling like an angry bear himself, Zeke dropped the rifle and unbuckled his gun belt, then glared at Brent.

Brent considered his alternatives. For the first time since coming to the canyon, he had the advantage. But he didn't see how he was going to profit from it. If Nanz and Dix weren't in the canyon, he could force Joel to turn Virgie over to him. But Lud and Starry were no match for Dix and Nanz. If Brent couldn't get Virgie soon, Lud and Starry would need the help of both Joel and Zeke to keep her safe from Dix and his killer.

'All right,' he said finally. 'Step in behind your pa, Zeke. Stand on the springs of that trap while he gets up.'

Zeke moved quickly to obey the command and Joel got up, heaving a great sigh of relief. Then his face clouded as he glared at Brent.

'Before you get any ideas,' Brent warned, 'remember, I've got the guns now. I'd make buzzard bait of you just like you aimed to do with me, except you may be needed to keep Dix and Nanz away from Virgie. You know, don't you, that you hired Dix's killer when you took on Nanz?'

Joel scowled but held himself in check in the face of the gun Brent was holding. 'We know it now,' he admitted.

'If you'll promise to leave me alone, I'll let you go,' Brent said. 'Otherwise, I'll tie you both up and set you on those traps again. There's another one over there for Zeke.'

Joel and Zeke exchanged glances then both nodded. 'We'll go after Dix and his gun hand,' Joel grumbled. 'We'll leave you alone.'

Brent didn't really believe him but he had to get some satisfaction out of his advantage. He couldn't kill them in cold blood. Besides, they would be a help in keeping Dix and Nanz at bay. If they got into a battle with Dix and Nanz, it might give Brent a chance to take Virgie and run.

Joel and Zeke looked longingly at their guns but Brent held the rifle on them. They left the cabin and started at a trot through the trees. Once they were out of sight, Brent gathered up the guns and went behind the burlap curtain and into the tunnel. There he left the two rifles and one revolver beside his sack of grub and buckled on Zeke's gun belt, making sure he had plenty of ammunition for the gun.

Back in the cabin, he checked the feel of the gun. It was good. He felt ready to meet any challenge now. The first challenge was to get Virgie out of that house. It would mean getting the drop on either Lud or Starry and using the threat of killing him to get Virgie away.

Leaving the cabin, he headed through the trees toward the Kurtzman place. He knew he'd have to beat Zeke and Joel there if he could. They'd have to travel carefully because they were unarmed and Dix and Nanz were somewhere around. Dix and his gunman wouldn't hesitate to kill either Joel or Zeke if they got the chance.

Brent was out of breath when he came in sight of the Kurtzman cabin. He paused there to size up the situation. He didn't see either

Starry or Lud outside the house as they had been this morning.

He guessed Joel and Zeke hadn't arrived yet. Joel, at least, could not have run that far. He was too old and too heavy for such running. Zeke was young enough but he had the same weight problem his father had.

'I've been looking for this chance,' someone said directly behind Brent.

Brent knew before he turned that it was Zeke. But Zeke couldn't have a gun yet. He whirled and saw his mistake again. Zeke and Lud were there and Zeke had Lud's gun.

Brent slowly let the gun in his hand fall. It had been that gun that had given him the confidence to rush up here. He had gotten careless and it had cost him his chance to get himself and Virgie out of the canyon.

CHAPTER THIRTEEN

Virgie was a prisoner in the house now. Joel had left explicit instructions for her to stay indoors, no matter what happened. With Lud in front of the house and Ike Starry at the rear, there certainly wasn't much chance of her getting outside for anything.

She tried to read but there was practically nothing around the house to read as none of the Kurtzmans cared to read much. Virgie's schooling wasn't doing her any good now, that was sure. She wandered from window to window, looking out and wondering what was going on. Joel and Zeke were out there somewhere looking for Dix. From what Brent had told her, Nanz was working for Dix. And, of course, they all would be looking for Brent as well. If they found any of them, they'd kill them. If any of the three came near the house, Lud and Starry had orders to kill them.

She wouldn't care if Joel found Dix or Nanz. Dix had frightened her more than any other man she had ever seen. She was convinced that he'd had every intention of killing her when Lud sneaked up and surprised him. She'd never seen such hate in a man's face as Dix had registered when he'd had to let Virgie go. Lud had proved himself a man in Virgie's eyes then. But she doubted if Joel would ever recognize it. He had lashed Lud with scorching words because he hadn't killed Dix when he had the chance. He didn't give Lud a word of praise for saving Virgie.

Then as she was passing the door, she noticed that Starry had moved around to the front of the house. Virgie moved across to the back and looked out the window to see if Lud was there. She saw him moving toward the trees behind the house. She wondered if Lud had gone to join Joel and Zeke in the search for the intruders, leaving Ike Starry the full responsibility of guarding the house.

Lud disappeared and Virgie wandered around the house again, returning to look at the spot where she had last seen Lud. She now saw him standing almost in the edge of the trees. She watched, fascinated by Lud's alertness as if he heard something.

Then she saw Zeke come up, holding his side as if he had an ache from running hard. Zeke and Lud talked for a minute, then both turned their attention to the trees. Zeke reached over and grabbed Lud's gun from him.

A moment later, Brent appeared not far from the brothers, his eyes on the house. Virgie almost screamed a warning to him even though she knew it'd do no good. She was inside the house and Brent was over two hundred yards away. He'd never hear her and even if he did, he wouldn't be able to escape Zeke and Lud now. They were too close to him.

She saw them surprise Brent and saw him drop the gun he held. Then the brothers marched Brent back into the trees. Virgie dropped in a chair close to the window, her breath coming in short gasps, as if the lump in her throat was preventing her from breathing.

Brent meant nothing to her, she tried to tell herself. But she knew it was a lie. He had offered her a hope that could lead her out of the canyon. He had even suggested that she wasn't a Kurtzman at all and no one yet had refuted that assumption to her satisfaction.

But there was something else about him. Brent was gentle. She hadn't known that quality here except perhaps at times when she had found Lud engrossed in his poetry. Gentleness was a vice that Joel didn't allow in his presence. Even Emma seemed hard and brittle when she was around Joel. But Brent was different. It wasn't a surface thing with him that could be wiped off in a moment. It came from deep inside. She felt it and was drawn to it.

Now she would know that gentleness no more, she was sure. Lud wouldn't kill Brent but Zeke would. In fact he would enjoy doing it just as Joel would. She knew Joel's orders were to kill Brent and Dix and Nanz whenever the opportunity appeared.

Emma hurried in from the kitchen. 'Did you see Zeke and Lud catch that stranger?' she asked.

Virgie nodded and didn't say anything. Emma looked out the window but Virgie knew there was nothing to see there now. She had watched as long as anyone was in sight.

'They won't kill him right away,' Emma said, as if to herself but Virgie had the feeling Emma had seen how this had struck her, and tried to offer some comfort without appearing to do it. 'Joel thinks he knows more about Dix than we do. He'll want to find out what he can.'

'Then Zeke will just hold him till Pa can talk

to him?' Virgie asked.

Emma nodded. 'That's how I figure it. If Pa wants to talk to the stranger and Zeke kills him first, I wouldn't want to be in Zeke's shoes.'

If that was know it was, Virgie wouldn't want to trade places with Zeke, either. But she wasn't sure that Joel's desire for information about Dix would overshadow his eagerness to see Brent dead.

A clump on the doorstep brought Virgie and Emma around to look at the front door. Joel stumbled through the door, his face red, puffing as though he'd been running for miles. He grabbed the back of the chair but he didn't turn it around and sit down. Instead, he staggered over to the corner where he kept his guns and began fumbling for a gun and ammunition.

'What happened, Joel?' Emma asked, moving half way across the room.

'I'll kill him!' Joel panted. 'I'm going to shoot off one finger at a time, poke out his eyes, cut out his tongue, and then kill him.'

Even Emma seemed taken aback by the fury in Joel's words. 'Who are you talking about? Dix?'

'That sneaking stranger who came in here first,' Joel got a gun, checked it for shells and found it empty. He cursed again and began filling the cylinder.

Tolly came running in. 'Did you get 'em,

Pa?' he asked eagerly.

Joel wheeled on Tolly like a wounded grizzly. 'You're the one who said you could turn that stranger over to me, and you didn't! It's your fault.'

Tolly backed off a step but fury surged up in his face, too. 'It ain't my fault. I told you you could have him but you wouldn't do what I asked you to.'

'So you turned him loose and he blamed near killed me!' Joel stormed across the room at Tolly. 'I ought to kill you.'

Before Tolly could dodge or Emma could stop him, Joel slammed a fist against the side of Tolly's head. Tolly staggered against the wall as if he'd been kicked by a mule. There he slowly slid to a sitting position against the wall.

'You got no call to do that,' Tolly screamed. 'I didn't turn him loose. He got loose by himself. You wouldn't dare hit me like that if Tolliver was here.'

'That's another thing,' Joel roared. 'I'm going to kill that dog.'

Tolly scrambled to his feet and ran out the door. 'You ain't either!' he screamed.

Joel wheeled on Emma and Virgie. 'Where's Zeke?'

'He caught the stranger you're looking for,' Emma said.

Joel's eyes lighted with a new fire. 'Where'd he take him?'

Emma didn't say anything for a moment

and Virgie answered. 'They went up the canyon,' she said. 'Lud was with them.'

'Lud ain't no help,' Joel said. He looked at Emma. 'Do you know where Zeke was taking him?'

Virgie looked at Emma. She would tell Joel the truth that Zeke and Lud had taken Brent down the canyon. She always told Joel the truth. Virgie had lied, hoping to give Brent just a little longer to live while Joel hunted for them.

'I don't know where they took him,' Emma said. 'Maybe up to Gunsight Rock.'

'Good,' Joel said. 'I'll catch them. And then I'll teach him to sit me on a bear trap.'

He stormed out the door. Virgie expected to hear the argument between Joel and Tolly renewed, maybe even a shot if Joel decided to kill Tolliver. But there was no argument outside. Joel evidently was too intent on getting his revenge on Brent. Brent had obviously done something to Joel and also taken his guns because Joel had to come home to get another one.

Virgie turned to Emma. 'Why did you tell him that, Ma?'

Emma turned to Virgie and she could see the fear in Emma's face. 'It was what you wanted, wasn't it?'

Virgie nodded numbly. 'But you never lied to Pa before. What'll he do when he finds out?'

'We'll climb that hill when we get to it,' Emma said.

Impulsively, Virgie moved over and hugged Emma, something she hadn't done in ten years.

'You've talked to him, haven't you?' Emma accused. 'He wants to take you away from here, doesn't he?'

Virgie nodded.

Emma sighed. 'I guess I knew it would happen some day. Some man is bound to get you.'

'It's not like that, Ma,' Virgie said quickly. 'But he has treated me nice. I—I just don't want him killed.'

A sob out in the yard tore Virgie's attention from Emma. 'I'm going out and talk to Tolly.'

'You do that,' Emma said. 'You can do more with him than anybody.'

Virgie ran outside. Tolly was in the pen with his dog, his arms around the dog's neck. That might have been why Joel hadn't stopped to kill the dog. He could hardly have shot the dog without hitting Tolly. Furious as he was, he wouldn't risk killing his own son.

'It's all right, Tolly,' Virgie said, crouching just outside the pen. 'Pa's gone. He'll forget about being mad when he comes back.'

'He ain't going to kill Tolliver,' Tolly sobbed. 'He can hit me but he ain't going to kill my dog.'

'He won't kill Tolliver,' Virgie said. 'He's

151

gone now. Better come on into the house.'

Tolly got up and looked up the canyon in the direction Joel had gone. 'I ain't going to leave Tolliver out here where Pa can get to him when I'm not watching.'

He opened the pen gate and let the dog outside. Then he followed Virgie into the house, the dog stopping right on the doorstep.

'Where's Pa going?' Tolly asked.

'Zeke caught the stranger and Pa was going to find them.'

Tolly looked back up the canyon. 'I was just up there. They ain't there.'

Virgie nodded. 'I know. They're down the canyon but Pa has to have time to cool off before he finds them.'

Tolly seemed to understand that. He followed Virgie inside, then went back and called Tolliver inside too. Emma looked suspiciously at the dog but Virgie reassured her.

'He won't bother anybody, Ma, unless Tolly tells him to. You know that.'

'I've always been afraid of that dog,' Emma said.

'Tolliver won't hurt you, Ma,' Tolly said. 'He knows I'd hurt him if he did.'

Ike Starry came in only a minute later. Emma frowned and Virgie went into the other room to be away from him.

'Do you think you can watch the house better from the inside?' Emma asked sarcastically.

'Ain't nobody going to bother this house,' Starry said. 'Not with Joel and Zeke and Lud roaming around, armed to the teeth.'

Virgie was aware that Starry had come on into the room where she was. When she looked up, she saw his gleaming eyes fastened on her.

'I hear you want to get out of the canyon,' Starry said. 'I'll take you out.'

Virgie saw that he meant it. He had evidently let a gnawing idea grow on him until he had reached the point where he was going to take the chance on doing what he'd been thinking of.

'I haven't told you I wanted to leave the canyon,' Virgie said.

'You don't have to put things into words,' Starry said, his big grin revealing teeth that were tobacco stained and broken into snags.

Virgie backed away in spite of herself. 'I'm not going anywhere,' she said.

'I made up my mind,' Starry said. 'I'm going to take you out of the canyon.'

Emma stepped into the room, her face red with anger. 'She said she wasn't going, Ike. Now you shut up. Joel will skin you alive if he finds out you even suggested it.'

'I ain't dealing with Joel,' Starry said. 'I'm talking to Virgie.'

'You just want her,' Emma said, fury building rapidly in her. 'You ain't caring

153

whether you get her out of the canyon or not.'

Starry looked at Emma for the first time. 'You'd best keep out of this. I'm taking Virgie out and there ain't nothing anybody can do about it.'

He stepped across the room quicker than Virgie had ever seen him move. Before she could dodge away, he had a grip on her arm and was starting to drag her to the door.

Suddenly Tolly appeared behind Emma with Tolliver at his side. The tear stains were still on his face but he was determined.

'You let her go, Ike,' he said. 'She's always good to me. If you don't, I'll turn Tolliver loose on you.'

This last threat seemed to get through to Starry. The threat of what Joel would do hadn't carried enough weight since he wasn't here. But Tolliver was right there and he was more than willing to make his presence felt.

'You keep that dog to yourself,' Starry growled, 'or I'll kill him.'

'You say that once more and I'll turn him loose,' Tolly threatened, his voice rising. 'I sure will.'

Starry gave another tug on Virgie's arm but his eyes were on the dog. Tolly stepped into the room and Tolliver moved with him, his gleaming eyes fastened on Starry. He seemed to know that Starry was his target, probably because even an animal could see that Virgie was being abused and Virgie was about the

154

only person who could get along with Tolliver other than Tolly.

'Just jerk on her once more and I let him go,' Tolly threatened.

Starry didn't doubt it. He dropped Virgie's arm. 'You and that dog are both going to be sorry,' he said and wheeled out the door. Tolliver growled after him.

'Good boy, Tolly,' Emma said. 'You did a man's job then.'

Tolly grinned, his tear streaked face beaming.

Virgie turned her eyes back to the window looking down the canyon. She couldn't see anything. She wondered how long it would be before Joel discovered that Zeke and Lud had taken their prisoner down the canyon instead of up. What could she do to save Brent from Joel's wrath? Or would Zeke kill him before Joel even found them? Time dragged.

'Hey in there!' a voice shouted from behind the barn.

'We've got the place surrounded. Send that girl out.'

'That's Dix,' Emma cried in alarm. 'I wish Joel was here now.'

'How can Dix surround the house himself?' Virgie asked, unable to keep the tremble of fear out of her voice.

'He's got that big man, Nanz, with him,' Emma said. 'And maybe somebody else by now. Joel hasn't kept anybody at the gap to

155

keep people out.'

Virgie knew she was right. Maybe Dix had brought in some of the cowboys. He was a big rancher, Emma said. She knew that this time, Dix would make certain she died before anybody could rescue her.

'I can slip you out the east window to the creek and up to my cave,' Tolly said.

Emma and Virgie both looked at the boy. He was serious. His mind seemed to be working well enough now. Virgie knew instantly that Tolly was offering her the only chance she had. It might not work but it was better than waiting here for Dix to come in and kill her.

'Let's go,' she said.

'I'll keep Dix busy,' Emma said, moving to the side of the house facing the sheep shed.

She yelled something at Dix and Dix answered. Virgie didn't pay any attention to the conversation. She was following Tolly, who moved fast now. Tolly went out the window and Tolliver leaped out after him. Then Virgie followed. Ducking low, they slipped into some bushes and made their way to the creek. Virgie expected someone to stop them but she realized that Dix was bluffing when he said he had the house surrounded. If that had been so, someone would have seen them.

Virgie had to lift her skirts and run hard to keep up with Tolly and the dog. Tolly knew they had no time to lose. He was excited because he was doing something that others approved of. But, he was forgetting that his mission was to protect Virgie and he set a pace she could barely match.

Somehow, though, she kept up and in a short time, they were even with Tolly's cave, and they followed the thin stand of trees up to the mine. Tolliver suddenly stopped and looked back, the bristles standing up on his neck. Tolly stopped, too, and turned back.

'Can you find the cave?' he whispered.

She nodded and he ran back over the tracks they had made coming up. Tolliver ran ahead of him. Virgie ducked behind the tree at the mouth of the cave and waited there. She heard a man yell and a dog bark and growl. There was running and then all was still.

After a while Tolly came. 'We scared the pants off Starry,' he said. 'He's joined up with Dix and that big fellow. But he won't be coming back up here. He's running yet, I reckon.'

'He won't come back as long as Tolliver is here, that's sure,' Virgie said.

'He ain't going to know that Tolliver ain't waiting for him,' Tolly said.

'You're not going to leave me, are you?' Virgie asked in alarm.

'Nobody'll find you here,' Tolly said. 'Nobody knows about this cave.'

'I knew about it,' Virgie said. 'If you take Tolliver away, they can get me without any trouble.'

Tolly shook his head stubbornly. 'They won't find this cave. Just stay out of sight.'

He turned and was gone like a shadow, the dog at his heels. Virgie almost cried. If they found her here, she'd be worse off than if she'd stayed at the house. At least, she had Emma there.

Tolly was sure they couldn't find her here. Virgie was almost equally sure that they could. If Ike Starry didn't know before where Tolly's hideout was, he surely did now. He had been following them. Tolliver had scared him back, but how long would he stay away? Or would he tell Dix where the mine was? It was Dix that Virgie was so frightened of, although she couldn't bear to think about Starry finding her here, either.

All she could do now was to be quiet and hope that Tolly was right in thinking they couldn't find her.

CHAPTER FOURTEEN

Brent had blamed his own carelessness for his predicament as he was marched back down the valley from the house. He'd had a gun; he'd almost reached the house where Virgie was; he'd had the upper hand for one of the few times since he'd come to the canyon. And he'd

158

gotten careless and let it all slip away. He had no illusions about his chances now.

Lud had picked up the gun Brent had dropped so now both Zeke and Lud were armed. Brent wondered how far they were going to take him. He didn't doubt that Zeke intended to kill him soon. He'd been trying for days and now he had the perfect opportunity.

'This is far enough,' Zeke said after just a short walk.

'Going to kill him here?' Lud asked.

'Going to wait for Pa,' Zeke said. 'Pa would peel our ears off if we killed him before he got a chance to work him over. Pa owes him something and I figure he's going to get a lot of pleasure out of paying it back.'

'Ain't killing him enough?' Lud asked, his face a little pale.

'Not for Pa,' Zeke said with relish. 'He set Pa on a bear trap and made him sit there still as a mouse while he took his guns.'

'He could've killed him, couldn't he?'

Zeke nodded. 'He could've killed both of us but he didn't. That was *his* big mistake.'

Lud was silent for a long time. Zeke leaned against a tree but his gun was always ready in case Brent made a break.

'How long'll we have to wait?' Lud asked.

'I figure Pa'll get home pretty soon. He can't run as fast as I can. When he gets home and finds out I haven't been there, he'll come back this way looking for me. I don't intend to be hard to find.'

When an hour went by and Joel hadn't shown up, Zeke began to get impatient. He sent Lud back to the house to find out if Joel had been there. When Lud got back, he was confused himself.

'Ma's the only one there,' he reported. 'She said Pa was there and went out looking for us. They saw us catch this fellow but thought we were going to take him up the canyon.'

'How could they think that when they saw us take him this way?' Zeke exploded. 'Who told him that? Virgie?'

'I don't know,' Lud said. 'Virgie ain't there, either. Dix came back and yelled for them to send Virgie out. Tolly slipped her out the window and took her some place to hide her. Ma's there alone.'

'Where's Dix?'

'Ma said she saw Ike talking to Dix out behind the sheep shed. Ike must have thrown in with Dix and Nanz. Maybe Ike knows where Tolly took Virgie. Anyway, they left and Ma hasn't seen anybody since.'

Zeke swore. 'They probably went up the canyon. Tolly spends a lot of time up there. That's probably where he hid Virgie. But Pa's up there, too. He may run into them.'

There was worry in Zeke's voice. Then suddenly he cocked his head to one side, listening. He pointed to Lud, then to Brent, and he slipped into the trees. Lud kept his gun on Brent.

Brent considered making a break. He'd have a much better chance getting away from Lud than Zeke. But Lud was desperate, too. He didn't like what he was involved in but there was a wild gleam in his eyes that told Brent he'd do anything to keep from running afoul of Joel's anger. Letting Brent get away would likely mean he'd be beaten if not killed.

Zeke was back in a minute with Joel trailing. Joel looked completely worn out. But at sight of Brent, his face turned red and the weariness melted from him.

'I've been waiting for this chance,' Joel said savagely. 'First, I want to know something. Why did you come here?'

Brent considered his answer carefully. 'I heard about Virgie being here and guessed who she was,' he said. 'I don't want Dix to get to her.'

'You know too much,' Joel growled. 'Who told you?'

'Lot of people know your secret,' Brent said.

'What do you know about Dix and Nanz?' Joel asked, breathing hard. 'Who is Nanz, anyway?'

'Dix's gun hand,' Brent said. 'They know about Virgie or they wouldn't be here.'

'What's this about Virgie, Pa?' Zeke asked. 'Is there something about her that you ain't told us?'

'Never mind about her,' Joel growled. 'We'll

take care of Dix and Nanz when we get through with this fellow.'

'What are you going to do, Pa?' Lud asked, looking like he wished he was somewhere else.

'First, I'm going to make him pay for that bear trap he set. Nobody sets Joel Kurtzman on a bear trap and lives to tell about it.'

Brent saw the fury building up in Joel. Still he wasn't prepared for the swiftness of his attack. His fist caught Brent on the side of the face and he reeled back against a tree, lost his balance, and spun around the tree to the ground.

He saw Joel charging toward him, aiming a kick at his face. He ducked farther behind the tree, throwing Joel's aim off so he missed his kick. It only infuriated Joel more. Scrambling to his feet, Brent dodged among the trees as Joel tried to catch him.

'Why don't you shoot him and be done with it?' Lud yelled.

'I ain't going to shoot him,' Joel panted. 'I'm going to beat him to death. He's going to be spread over this whole area like grease on a skillet.'

Joel hit Brent again but Brent kept his feet and dodged away, catching Joel a glancing blow of his own. That was when Zeke stepped in.

'You try hitting Pa again,' Zeke yelled, 'and I'll put a bullet in your foot so you can't run.'

Whether he fought back or not, Brent knew

he was going to be beaten to death. There was a sadistic streak in both Joel and Zeke that made them enjoy every minute of something like this. He almost wished he had the same temperament. If he had, he wouldn't be in this fix now. He'd have butchered both of them back at the cabin. But he knew he couldn't have done it even if he'd known what was coming. It just wasn't in him.

Joel kept charging and Brent dodged back and forth, trying to keep trees between him and Joel. Even when Joel got in a blow, it usually had less force than the big man expected because of his weariness.

'Want me to take him a while Pa?' Zeke asked eagerly.

'Not till I show him who he set on that bear trap,' Joel said determinedly.

Brent went down again from a sledge hammer blow that Joel landed. He tried to roll away from the kick that Joel aimed at his head and barely managed to get out of the way. But he was against a tree and Joel wheeled, seeing the advantage he had been seeking all along. His face spread in a vicious grin as he charged at Brent.

'Stop it!' someone screamed hysterically.

The yell was so shrill that even Joel wheeled to see who had interfered. Tolly was standing twenty feet away, a hand gripping the leash on the dog. Most of the time Tolliver ran loose in the trees with Tolly but he wasn't loose now.

'You keep out of this, Tolly!' Joel roared.

'Stop hitting him,' Tolly yelled.

'You shut up!' Joel roared and turned back toward Brent who had scrambled to his feet now.

'If you hit again, I'll turn Tolliver loose,' Tolly threatened.

'Turn him loose,' Joel yelled. 'I've been wanting to kill him, anyway.'

Joel concentrated on Brent then. Brent half dodged his charge but the blow sent him reeling backward, anyway. Out of the corner of his eye, he saw Tolliver break loose. He doubted if Tolly had actually let him go.

Zeke saw the dog, too, and wheeled, firing his gun and missed the dog by a foot. Joel heard the shot and spun around. Then, without trying to grab his gun, he turned and ran, showing a fear of the dog that he didn't have for any human. Zeke fired again, missed again and then he, too, turned and ran. Lud simply faded back into the trees. The dog was concentrating on the two who had mistreated him so much.

Tolly called Tolliver back after Joel and Zeke had disappeared into the trees. Then he came to Brent.

'Did he hurt you much?'

Brent moved around gingerly. 'I'm all in one piece. Thanks for the help, Tolly.'

'He hadn't ought to have done what he did,' Tolly said, embarrassed at the thanks. 'You want to see Virgie?'

Brent nodded. 'I sure do.'

Tolly didn't say anything, just turned and headed up the valley, detouring to the west canyon wall around the home buildings. Brent followed. He guessed Tolly was taking him to his cave. That's the only place that Brent could think of where Tolly would try to hide Virgie.

Brent had a sinking feeling in the pit of his stomach all the way up the canyon. If Virgie knew about Tolly's cave, likely others did, too. Some of them might have found her by now.

Tolly moved quickly and Brent had to hurry to keep up. Without a word, Tolly went past the tree into the mine tunnel and Brent followed. Tolly stopped just inside without lighting the candle. Brent couldn't see into the tunnel at all.

'Virgie?' Tolly called softly.

'I'm here,' she said. 'I wasn't sure who was coming.'

She came back in the tunnel.

'I told you nobody would find you here,' Tolly said.

'Don't you see now that you have to get out of the canyon?' Brent asked.

'There are people like Dix and Nanz outside the canyon,' Virgie said.

'Those are the only two people who live out there who'd hurt you,' Brent said. 'They came in here to kill you. If you were out there, you'd be safe.'

'Are you going outside?' Tolly asked in bewilderment.

'If I do,' Virgie said, 'you can come out and visit me.'

Tolly's face lighted up. 'That'll be great. I'll help you get out.'

'Will you go, Virgie?' Brent pressed.

'Maybe,' she said hesitantly. 'I'm not safe here.'

'I'll have to get a gun,' Brent said. 'It's not likely we can get out of here without using a gun to scare somebody, at least.'

'You'd better shoot those two big fellows,' Tolly said.

Brent nodded. 'May have to.' He turned to Virgie. 'You wait here, Virgie. I'll go back to that old cabin where I put my stuff. I've got another gun there. I'll come right back and get you. We'll try to slip out tonight.'

'All right,' Virgie said. She touched his arm. 'Be careful. They all want to kill you.'

'I know.' He quieted his racing blood. It was the first time she had touched him voluntarily and it stirred him more than anything had ever done before.

Turning quickly, he moved back to the tree. From there, he surveyed the canyon in both directions. Everything appeared quiet. The sun was almost tipping the western rim of the canyon. Days were short down here in the bottom. But the twilight would last long as the sun hit the eastern wall and reflected into the canyon.

It wasn't the coming of night that fostered the urgency in him. He knew that every minute he stayed in this canyon he was running the risk of being killed. And the same was true for Virgie.

Leaving the mine entrance, he scurried down into the trees, then across into the aspens along the foot of the east wall. There he turned north toward the cabin in front of the mine. He half expected to run across some of the men looking for him but he got to the cabin without seeing a soul. He lost no time inside the cabin, going behind the burlap curtain and into the mine tunnel. He debated about taking a rifle but decided against it. He needed to travel light because he and Virgie would have to move fast to get out of the canyon alive.

He went back toward Tolly's cave the same way he had come. But halfway between the two tunnels, still in the aspens on the east side of the creek, he was surprised by a shot that slapped into a tree only inches from his shoulder.

In a headlong dive, he slid behind three trees that were growing close together. Scrambling to his feet, he peered between the trunks, trying to see who was shooting at him. It would have to be Dix or Nanz or the Kurtzmans. But he got a shock when he saw that the head inching up behind some bushes down next to the creek was Ike Starry's.

'Who you shooting at?' Brent yelled.

'You,' Starry yelled back. 'I'll get you, too. You ain't got no rifle.'

Brent hadn't expected Starry to take up Joel's fight. 'What's Kurtzman paying you for this?' he called back.

'Nothing,' Starry said. 'Dix is paying me—better than Joel ever paid me for anything.'

Brent watched Starry as he moved up closer to the trees. Starry knew he could safely move closer because Brent didn't have a rifle. Brent ducked away from the trees where he was hiding and, keeping low, angled on a course that would intercept Starry. Careful that Starry didn't see him, he cut the distance between them to less than half of what it had been when Starry had fired that first shot.

Before Brent wanted to be seen, however, Starry stopped and searched the trees ahead where he thought Brent was. Suddenly he saw Brent much closer and within range of a six-gun. Yelling in surprise and anger at being caught in this position, he jerked up his rifle and pumped two quick shots at Brent. Neither came close for Starry hadn't taken time to aim.

Brent swung his revolver up and fired. The bullet spun Starry around but it didn't stop him from coming up to one knee to shoot again. Being hit seemed to knock the panic out of him and he deliberately took aim for his next shot. Brent didn't wait but sent two more quick shots at Starry.

He knew that part of his accuracy was luck for Starry was still at long range for a revolver. However, his second shot sent Starry over backward and Brent knew he wouldn't get up.

Brent had started on toward the tunnel where Virgie waited when he realized just how small the canyon really was. He saw two big men crossing the little creek well down in front of him. Maybe Dix and Nanz had just happened to be close when the shooting started but if they hadn't been, they had covered a lot of territory in fast time.

Wheeling, Brent dodged back through the trees then saw Joel and Zeke down to his left. With Nanz and Dix behind him and the Kurtzmans on his left, he had only two courses left open to him. He could go straight ahead or swing back through the trees next to the canyon wall and posssibly get past Nanz and Dix. But if he did that, he'd almost certainly lead them to Virgie's hiding place. He wasn't going to risk that.

He ran hard, straight down the canyon, dodging among the trees. He didn't think the Kurtzmans had seen him. But looking back, he saw that Dix and Nanz had, and were running hard after him. His only chance, other than fighting it out with the two big men, was to get to that cabin and disappear into the tunnel behind the burlap curtain. He could see that Dix, at least, had a rifle. Brent wouldn't be as lucky against Dix and Nanz as he had been against Starry. He had to run.

Reaching the cabin out of breath, he dived inside and looked back out the glassless window. He didn't see anyone at first, then he saw the two men puffing through the trees. They surely hadn't seen him come into the cabin but they wouldn't see him going on down the canyon, either, so they might assume that he'd gone into the cabin.

Lifting the burlap curtain, Brent felt his way into the tunnel mouth and crawled in. Picking up the two rifles and all the ammunition he had taken from Joel and Zeke, he moved back. If Dix or Nanz tried to smoke him out of the tunnel, he'd make a good account of himself.

Sitting silently, he listened and was rewarded by the thump of boots on the cabin floor. Dix and Nanz had come into the cabin. Brent was too far back in the tunnel to hear what the two men were saying if they were talking. They might suspect that a tunnel existed behind the burlap curtain, but they didn't try to tear down the curtain to get at him. Brent was prepared for just such a move and, if they suspected he was there, they probably also suspected he'd be ready to greet them if they exposed the tunnel.

They left the cabin and Brent waited. They might just lie in wait outside until he ventured out. Then they'd shoot him like a fish in a barrel. He decided to wait until dark. He might slip past them then even if they were watching.

For a half hour he sat there waiting, guessing how dark it was getting outside. Then suddenly he heard a terrific rumble, followed by the splintering of boards. Dust puffed back into the tunnel.

Leaping up, Brent moved in a crouching run under the low ceiling toward the front of the tunnel. He reached the burlap and found it torn. But more important, he found the tunnel completely blocked by a mass of rocks. Dix and Nanz must have crawled above the cabin and started a rockslide that had demolished the cabin and blocked the tunnel. Brent knew from pushing on the rocks that he could never dig his way out of this.

CHAPTER FIFTEEN

Virgie heard the rifle shot and she ran to the mouth of the mine tunnel. She didn't even look outside, however, until she heard more rifle shots, echoed by the flatter reports of a six-gun. Peeking around the tree, she tried to see what was happening. But she couldn't see anything.

Shadows from the west wall covered the floor of the canyon. The shooting was down the canyon and across on the east side of the creek. She had to know what was happening so she moved away from the mine entrance and down into the trees along the river. Before she reached them, however, she saw two big men crossing the creek. They were too tall for Kurtzmans; they must be Dix and Nanz.

She considered slipping back into the cave but she saw that they were going down the canyon. They wouldn't see her. She was sure that Brent was either dead now or running the other way. He wouldn't come back to Tolly's cave to get her. The safest place for her was back at the house with Emma. If Tolly and his dog were here now, she'd stay and let them protect her. But she was alone. If Dix or Nanz found her, she'd be killed in a minute.

She fairly flew down the creek and reached the house without seeing anybody. There were no more shots across the creek. She couldn't rid herself of the feeling that Brent was in serious trouble. He should have been coming toward Tolly's cave when the shooting broke out. He was surely involved and he wouldn't stand much chance against all the men who were out to kill him.

Emma was alone in the house when she burst in, panting. She ran to meet Virgie and hugged her like she hadn't expected to see her alive again. Virgie's first impulse was to tell her about Brent and his promise to get her out of the canyon but she checked herself. Emma considered all the intruders in the canyon a threat to her family, especially Virgie.

Emma held Virgie tight for a minute. When she stepped back, Virgie saw the worry on her face. She'd heard the shooting, too, and wasn't sure what had happened.

'They must've killed that stranger or have him trapped,' Emma said. 'Or maybe it was that man, Dix.'

Virgie shook her head. 'I saw Dix and Nanz after the shooting was over.'

'Then it must be the stranger. But Dix is the biggest threat to us.'

'Ike Starry is helping Dix now,' Virgie said.

'The ungrateful dog!' Emma exploded. 'Joel takes him in so he won't spend the rest of his life in prison and that's how he pays us back.'

'Where's Tolly?' Virgie asked.

'Out looking for the intruders, too, I reckon,' Emma said. 'Joel and Zeke and Lud are all hunting. Sounded like they might have found one of them. Maybe the shooting will attract the others and they can clean out the whole outfit before dark.'

'If they don't get killed doing it,' Virgie said. 'I'm afraid of those two big men, Dix and Nanz.'

Emma nodded and walked to the window to look out. 'They're here for no good.'

The room grew quiet as deep dusk settled down. There were no more shots. If Brent hadn't been killed in that first exchange of shots, then he might still be alive. The very fact that there had been no more shots worried Virgie. It likely meant that the battle had ended with one combatant dead and there was no more need for fighting.

'Here comes Tolly,' Emma said at last from the window. 'Maybe he knows what went on. It's about dark. The others ought to be coming in.'

Virgie went to the window, too. In the deepening darkness, she could see Tolly and his dog coming up from the creek. From the direction he was approaching, she couldn't guess whether he had been up the canyon or down. He was running in his peculiar lope, which meant he was probably excited.

Tolly stopped long enough to put Tolliver in his pen not far from the door; then he burst into the house.

'Did you hear the shooting?' he demanded.

'Who was it?' Emma asked softly.

Her tone of voice drained some of the excitement out of Tolly but he was still bubbling with information that he wanted to share faster than his tongue could handle it.

'That was Ike fighting with the stranger, Brent,' he said.

Virgie felt herself go cold. Yet Tolly didn't seem depressed and he was more friendly with Brent than anyone he had ever known. Brent must not have lost the battle.

'How did the fight come out?' Virgie asked when Tolly seemed to be having trouble sorting out the words he wanted to say. Virgie's question straightened out his thinking.

'Brent killed Ike. Ike shot enough times but he couldn't hit anything. Brent just took his time and shot straight.'

'Can't say I'm sorry Ike got it,' Emma said, 'not after the way he double-crossed us. Where did Brent go?'

'That was quite a chase,' Tolly said. 'Those two big fellows took after him. Pa and Zeke and Lud were down in the trees but they didn't get started in time to see which direction the others went.'

'Where did they go?' Virgie asked impatiently.

'Those big fellows chased Brent down the canyon and Brent went into that old cabin down there. The big fellows charged in there but there wasn't no shooting. Then they came out and climbed up above the cabin. They kicked some rocks loose and started a rockslide. It came down on the cabin with a bang.'

Tolly was swinging his arms wildly, trying to emphasize the force with which the rocks hit the cabin.

'What happened to Brent?' Virgie asked, ununaware of the sharp glance that Emma gave her.

'He's buried under those rocks,' Tolly said. 'If he ain't dead, he's trapped. I'm going to dig him out and see.'

Tolly turned toward the door but Emma stopped him. 'You stay here, Tolly. It's dark out there. You can't see to do anything till morning. If he's dead, it won't make any difference anyway.'

'If he ain't, he may be hurting,' Tolly said.

Virgie knew that Tolly dreaded hurting more than anything. He didn't care what happened to those he didn't like but he didn't want anyone or anything that he loved to be hurting. He obviously had an affection for Brent.

'As long as he's hidden by those rocks, Dix and Nanz can't get to him to kill him,' Emma said.

Tolly considered that for a moment then nodded slowly. 'Hadn't thought of that. Maybe he's safer under the rocks than if I dug him out.'

'He will be till morning anyway,' Emma said.

There was still some light lingering in the canyon and a three-quarter moon was hanging over the east rim. The canyon wouldn't be totally dark tonight. Virgie had gone to the window to stare across the darkened valley toward the east wall, wondering if Brent was dead or alive. She had thought he would've been killed in the gunfire but he had survived that. Now he was buried under that rockslide. But the cabin was built right against the wall. Maybe the rocks had bounced out away from

176

the wall as they fell. They might've collapsed the cabin and still have left a fairly large breathing space between the place where they came to rest and the canyon wall. Brent would be safe in there. She would go there at first light tomorrow morning and see. She couldn't tell anybody her plans because then she wouldn't be allowed to go.

She saw Joel come puffing up from the trees along the creek. She knew it was Joel from the short quick strides he took. Zeke was almost the same size but he took longer steps.

'Pa's coming,' Virgie announced.

Tolly got up and headed for the far side of the cabin. Virgie saw the panic in his face and wondered what he had done to make him so afraid of Joel. Before he could find a place to hide, Joel stormed in through the front door.

'Somebody shook loose a rock slide over yonder,' Joel growled. 'Wrecked that old cabin. Figured the boys and me would save those logs one of these days. I'll bet it was Dix who did it.'

Joel's eyes flashed over the room; taking in everything in the light of the two candles Emma had lit. When he saw Tolly, his face flushed beet red and he swallowed hard before he could say anything.

'I didn't think you'd have nerve enough to come home, even for eating.' he grated.

'What's the matter, Joel?' Emma asked sharply. 'What's Tolly done?'

'He turned that hell-hound of his loose on me and Zeke when we had that stranger dead to rights.'

'He was beating him—fit to kill him,' Tolly said.

'That's what I was aiming to do,' Joel roared. 'After he set me on that bear trap, he deserved to be beaten to death, inch by inch.' He started across the room for Tolly. 'I'll learn you not to butt into things that ain't none of your business.'

Tolly stood against the wall, trembling. Virgie wanted to help him because Joel was in a terrible rage. But if she interfered, she would be smashed by his fury, too.

Just before Joel reached Tolly, his fist balled to hit him, Tolly ducked under Joel's arm and ran to the door. Joel wheeled and was only a step behind him going through the door. For a big man, he moved fast. Right now, he was driven by an uncontrollable rage. Emma rats to the door after him.

'Joel!' she screamed. 'Don't you touch him till you cool down.'

Joel ignored Emma. If Tolly had been content to leave his dog in the pen, he could have escaped Joel. But Tolly likely knew that Joel would kill the dog if he didn't get to vent his wrath on Tolly.

Tolly had just stopped at the gate when Joel caught up with him. Joel grabbed him by the shoulder and jerked him away with such force that he flew ten feet before hitting the ground. Joel wheeled and was after him like a cat after a mouse. Tolly tried to get to his feet but Joel's fist caught him on the side of the face as he was halfway up. The blow sent him rolling six feet farther away.

'I'll learn you!' Joel screamed.

Emma was wringing her hands. 'He's going to kill him. He's so mad he don't know what he's doing.'

Tolly was also sure that Joel was going to kill him. He scrambled away from Joel's rush as fast as he could. When he saw he couldn't get away, he started screaming for Tolliver.

The dog began leaping against the boards of his pen, barking and whining in a frenzy. Again and again he flung himself against the boards. But the pen was solid.

Joel slammed another fist into Tolly's face and Tolly rolled away to the edge of the yard. From here the ground dropped away sharply to the creek. Tolly kept screaming for Tolliver. The dog, finding he couldn't break down the gate, changed his tactics. He leaped toward the top of the fence that held him in. He fell back heavily the first time. On the second jump, he caught his front paws over the top of the fence. With his back feet clawing into the wood, Tolliver heaved himself up until his chest went over the fence. His back feet caught the top of the fence and he launched himself like a rocket toward the scene of the fight.

179

Joel had Tolly down now and was pounding him with all the fury of a maniac. He didn't even see the dog coming. Tolliver charged straight into Joel with the force of a runaway ox. Joel was a big man but Tolliver knocked him completely off Tolly. Joel landed on his side and then he saw what had hit him.

Joel's fury was matched only by the rage of the big dog. The dog had recognized the terror in his master's voice and this man was the cause of it.

Joel was no match for the dog. He tried to get his feet but the dog grabbed an arm and ripped away the sleeve and some of the flesh. Joel screamed, probably more from the realization of what was going to happen to him than from the pain of his wound.

Virgie watched the battle in the dim moonlight, spellbound by its horror. There was no doubt of the outcome unless Tolly stopped it. And right now Tolly was just beginning to stir, after having been knocked almost senseless by Joel. Another minute and Joel would have killed Tolly. Now in less than a minute, Tolliver was going to kill Joel unless somebody stopped him.

Joel screamed for somebody to get the dog off him. Emma started into the yard and stopped. She knew she couldn't do anything with Tolliver. Tolly was the only human alive who could stop him now. And Tolly was too far gone to realize what was happening.

Joel screamed another time or two, then stopped. A human voice can't escape from a throat gripped in the vise-like jaws of a fury-driven dog.

Virgie, sickened by the sight, turned back into the house, a lump in her throat so large that she could neither throw up nor swallow. Emma came to her in a minute and put an arm around her, sobs shaking her own body. She didn't say anything.

'Tolly,' Virgie whispered finally. 'He's hurt bad.'

Emma nodded. 'Got to take care of Tolly. Joel—' Tears drowned her words.

Virgie was surprised that Emma could feel such a loss for Joel when he had treated her only a little better than he had Tolly. It was probably more the shock of losing something on which she had leaned exclusively for twenty-five years, and the horror of the way Joel had met his end.

Virgie dreaded going back to the door. She'd never rid herself of the sight of that dog destroying Joel. But Tolly was out there and he needed help. She staggered across to the door. Emma followed.

Tolly was on his feet and he was staring at Joel, realization of what happened slowly taking hold of him. He looked at Tolliver, blood still clinging to his jaws. Then he turned and ran past the sheep shed into the trees. Tolliver went with him. Virgie started to follow him but Emma caught her arm. Her voice was fairly steady now.

'We have to let him go, Virgie,' she said. 'That's the worst shock he's ever had. He'll have to work it out by himself. No telling how he might react if one of us interfered.'

'What—what can we do?' Virgie whispered.

'Nothing now,' Emma said, wiping her nose then taking a deep breath. 'There've been times when I wanted to kill Joel myself after he beat me. But I never thought I'd see anything as awful as that.'

Neither Virgie nor Emma went outside. Within ten minutes Zeke and Lud came. Zeke stopped in the yard and his howl reminded Virgie of a wounded wolf. He charged into the house.

'It was that dog wasn't it?'

He wheeled back toward the door but Emma's sharp words stopped him. 'Joel brought it on himself. He was in one of his black rages. He was killing Tolly when the dog got out. Nobody could've stopped him but Tolly and he was already knocked out.'

Zeke and Lud took care of Joel's body, wrapping it and putting it in one corner of his bedroom until it could be buried tomorrow. Virgie, as sick as she could ever remember being, went to her room. But there was no sleep for her. Her mind kept returning to Joel's death. She tried to turn her thoughts to other things: at dawn she'd go to the cabin

182

buried under the rocks and see if she could find Brent. The thought of rescuing Brent was about the only thing that helped her keep her sanity through the long night.

Before dawn she slipped out of the house. She saw that the light was strong on the west face of the canyon wall, it'd be daylight before long. She continued cautiously past the shed where Tolly milked the cow and headed down to the creek. She knew where the cabin was. She wanted to get there before anyone discovered she was missing from the house.

She hurried through the trees along the creek. It was probably her haste that caused her to be careless. She'd almost forgotten that there were still enemies in the canyon. After Joel's death last night, it seemed to her that the entire world changed.

But she was brought back to reality with a jolt as a big man stepped in front of her as she was running with her head down, watching where she was going. She stopped, her eyes whipping up to see Murdo Nanz grinning at her.

'Been looking for you,' he said. 'But I sure didn't expect you to come running to me.'

Virgie wheeled but he anticipated the move and lunged forward, catching her arm before she could take a step.

'Now this is what I call real good luck,' Nanz said. 'I'm supposed to wait here for Jarron but I think we'll move up the creek a little. No use in letting him know that I've already got the prize.'

Virgie knew that Nanz was talking about Dix. She didn't want Dix to see her, that was sure. But she didn't feel much safer with Murdo Nanz. At the moment, however, there wasn't anything she could do but follow his instructions. His big hand on her arm was like a vise.

Nanz took her about a hundred yards up the creek and stopped in a dense thicket. 'We'll wait here till we get a chance to get out of this canyon,' Nanz said. He looked Virgie over, a wolfish grin on his face. 'I reckon you'd rather be alive than dead. If Dix gets you, you know what'll happen. But with me, you'll stay alive. I like you that way.'

Virgie felt the revulsion surge up in her. She wasn't sure she wouldn't prefer the death Dix had planned for her.

CHAPTER SIXTEEN

Brent had seldom felt as hopeless as he did when he faced that pile of rocks blocking the tunnel. He wasn't in immediate danger of being killed like he had been when Tolly had him tied to that unstable pole holding up the ceiling in the back of his tunnel, but his chances of escape from here were even less.

Who would know he was here except the men who had started the rockslide? They certainly wouldn't dig him out. There was no telling how many tons of rocks were between him and freedom. Maybe Dix and Nanz hadn't been able to start too big a slide, but it sure had sounded like a big one to Brent.

He tried pushing the rocks and found that he couldn't budge them. He did manage to pull a few of the smaller rocks from the pile directly in front of the tunnel mouth and lay them back in the tunnel. But that seemed like a hopeless task. Too many of the rocks were wedged into the pile so tightly he couldn't even wiggle them.

He didn't know what time it was but it had to be night. It had been almost dark when he'd run in here. It would be a long night and morning wouldn't bring any light to him.

He worked at the rocks, digging one loose now and then, until he got so tired he could hardly lift a hand, his fingers bleeding from tearing at the rocks. He finally stretched out to rest on the floor behind the little pile of rocks he had taken from the wedge.

He didn't know how long he slept but he felt much better when he awoke. His problem still faced him, however. He went back to the wedge and felt around for a rock that he could wiggle loose. He had prized a half-dozen rocks loose from the rubble when he thought he heard a sound outside. He paused and listened intently.

He heard the sound again and he stopped digging. About the only persons he could think of who might come back to make sure he was dead were Dix and Nanz. He didn't want them to find out he was still alive.

There was some hard clawing on the other side of the rock pile and he realized that the rock barrier was not as thick as he had figured. Then he heard a half whine, half growl— Tolly's dog! He waited a moment longer then heard Tolly call.

'Tolliver! Where are you?' His voice sounded far away.

The dog gave a sharp yelp, then went back to digging. Brent waited, listening, trying to determine what was going on outside. Then he heard Tolly just outside, probably beside Tolliver.

'Is he in there Tolliver?' Tolly said.

'I'm here,' Brent shouted.

'Are you all right, Brent?' Tolly called back.

'Sure,' Brent said. 'Just tired of being cooped up.'

'We'll get you out.'

Brent could hear rocks tumbling around as Tolly began moving them. Brent tried to help from the inside but he realized the progress he was making would hardly be recognizable compared to what Tolly could do out there where he could see.

When Tolly paused to rest, Brent asked a

question. 'How'd you know I was in here?'

'I saw those big men push the rocks down on the cabin,' Tolly said. 'I figured you was dead or trapped. Tolliver found you.'

Tolly went to work again and Brent loosened what rocks he could from the inside. Then Tolly moved a rock and Brent could see daylight. He clawed at the rocks around the opening and enlarged the hole. Tolly moved another rock and the hole was almost big enough for Brent to get his head through. A few more rocks and Brent squeezed his shoulders through the hole, dragging himself out into the open.

He saw then that most of the rocks had crashed down onto the cabin. The cabin roof had shunted them outward when it collapsed. A small pile had dropped straight down after the cabin roof had pulled away, blocking the entrance to the tunnel. Tolly had been outside the main pile of rocks when Tolliver had slipped under the collapsed roof and caught Brent's scent at the tunnel mouth.

Tolly didn't say a word but turned and crawled back under the roof to the outside. Brent followed him, noticing that something was wrong with Tolly. Once out from under the sagging roof, Brent realized that it wasn't just morning; it was late in the forenoon. The sun was hitting the valley floor.

'Where is Virgie?' he asked.

Tolly looked at him, his eyes wild. There

were tear streaks down his cheeks and two big purple bruises covered a swelled area on one side of his jaw.

'She's home, I reckon,' Tolly mumbled.

'What happened to you, Tolly?' Brent asked, moving closer.

Tolly shrank back. 'I got to go. You'd best get out of here.'

Brent frowned. Somebody had beaten Tolly unmercifully but he wasn't going to tell who. From the wildness in his eyes, Brent guessed that the memory of it was more than his mind could bear.

Before Brent could say any more, Tolly turned and ran down the slope, disappearing into the trees, Tolliver just one lope behind him. Something traumatic had happened to Tolly since Brent had been locked in that mine. He wished he knew what it was.

Brent still had his gun and checked it. He hadn't reloaded it since he'd had that fight with Ike Starry. Quickly he attended to that. He thought of going back into the tunnel and getting one of the rifles that he'd taken from Joel and Zeke but decided against it. One thing Tolly had said made sense—he'd better get out of the canyon as quickly as possible.

He followed Tolly down the slope into the trees by the creek and turned up the canyon toward the main ranch buildings. Tolly had said he thought Virgie was at home. But Tolly hadn't looked as if he had slept in a bed last night. Maybe he hadn't been home so he didn't know where she was.

Remembering the way he'd been caught yesterday by being careless, he proceeded cautiously up the creek bank, his eyes searching for any movement. If Virgie was still in the canyon, then it was a good bet that Dix and Nanz were, too. There were just two days left now until the hearing in Greeley. If Dix could make sure Virgie didn't get to Greeley in the next two days, he'd get Pool ranch.

He was over halfway to the house when he caught a movement off to his right in the trees. He stepped over against a tree and tried to melt into the trunk while he watched. He saw another man moving in the same direction he was going, apparently intent on getting up close to the house, too. He hadn't seen Brent so Brent had the advantage of surprise. But the surprise was more on Brent's side as he recognized the man.

Brent slipped away from the tree where he'd been standing and moved over behind the other man.

'Frank,' he said softly. The other man stopped, hand poised above gun. 'Don't get jumpy. It's Brent.'

Frank Zarada turned, a big grin easing the tension in his face. 'I was hoping you'd be here,' he said, walking over to Brent. 'But I was expecting Kurtzman or one of his boys.'

'They're around, I reckon,' Brent said. 'Dix

and Nanz are here, too.'

Zarada nodded. 'I know. That's why I came. They forced their way into my house the day you slipped out and beat the information out of me about Virgie. I came as soon as I felt up to it. Figured you might need some help in getting her out of here.'

'That's no lie,' Brent said. 'Dix and Nanz shoved a rockslide down on the cabin where I was hiding out last night. If it hadn't been for the youngest Kurtzman boy, I'd be locked in that mine tunnel behind the cabin yet.'

'The crazy one, Tolly?' Zarada asked.

Brent nodded. 'I guess he's off mentally, all right. But he thinks I'm his friend and he and his dog found me this morning and dug me out.'

Zarada showed surprise. 'I didn't suppose anybody could make up to Tolly. What about Joel and the other two?'

'Around here somewhere. They're probably hunting Dix and Nanz as well as me. They'll kill any one of us they find.'

'That figures,' Zarada said. 'Have you talked with Virgie?'

Brent nodded. 'Had her talked into going out of the canyon with me. Then I got into a fight with Kurtzman's hired hand, Starry. I bested him, but then Dix and Nanz ran me into that cabin and pushed the rocks down on it.'

'If Virgie's willing to go with you, then

190

about all you have to do is find her. There's nobody at the mouth of the canyon now. I came in that way. I knew Dix came that way. I thought if he could get in, I could, too.'

'Nanz helped Dix get in,' Brent said. 'I was on my way up toward the house now to see if I could find Virgie. Maybe you should come along.'

'Good idea,' Zarada agreed. 'I'll serve as a guard while you sneak in and get her.'

Brent moved ahead then and Zarada followed, staying well behind him. Getting Virgie out of that house was not going to be easy, even with Zarada guarding the escape route.

He hurried forward and was well out in front of Zarada when he heard a scream off to his left. It lasted only a second and was suddenly stifled. Brent hardly had time to identify or locate it but it had sounded like a woman's scream. That would mean either Virgie or Emma. And Brent was sure nobody would bother Emma.

He ducked under a tree branch and ran toward the sound. It had come from across the creek, he thought. What would Virgie be doing out here? And what had caused her to scream? Even more important, what had stopped her scream so quickly?

Brent lifted his gun from the holster and moved ahead swiftly but cautiously. He'd been surprised too often already in this canyon.

Then he caught a glimpse of a big man through the trees ahead. He stopped, hidden behind a tree. He recognized Murdo Nanz who was holding Virgie with one arm, looking around in all directions. Apparently, he was wondering if anyone had heard Virgie's short scream.

Brent waited until Nanz moved ahead, pulling Virgie with him. He saw that Nanz was heading for the lower end of the canyon. Apparently, he knew that no one was guarding the gap now.

Brent crossed the creek and ran down the canyon again, paralleling the course he thought Nanz was taking. He had to get to the gap before Nanz did. If Nanz got Virgie out of the canyon, it wasn't likely he'd ever see her alive again. He was surprised that Nanz hadn't killed her as soon as he caught her.

Brent wondered about Zarada trying to follow him to the house. If he had heard the scream, too, he likely would know what it meant and also would be following Nanz. But if he hadn't, he'd go on toward the house and Brent would have to rescue Virgie by himself.

He couldn't charge right at Nanz. Nanz would certainly kill Virgie or use her as a shield while he shot Brent. He'd have to find some other way to get at Nanz without jeopardizing Virgie's life. It struck Brent suddenly that Nanz probably wanted Virgie for himself and that was why he hadn't killed her.

If that was the case, Nanz would be dodging Dix, too. Dix wanted Virgie dead, nothing else.

Brent reached the narrows where the creek plunged through the gap. There were few trees here. He scanned the space ahead. Nanz wasn't in sight. Unless he had gotten out of the canyon ahead of Brent, Nanz had to be somewhere behind him. Turning, Brent found a spot from which he could see anyone coming down the canyon.

He was just ducking into the hiding spot he'd selected when he saw Nanz coming, still dragging Virgie. Brent dropped down quickly but he knew it hadn't been fast enough. Nanz stopped dead in his tracks then jerked Virgie around in front of him.

For a minute, Brent thought Nanz was going to try to bull his way through the gap, using Virgie as a shield. But he evidently thought better of it and turned back instead, moving away at a slow trot. Brent wondered if Nanz had thought that the man waiting for him was Dix. Dix wouldn't hesitate an instant to shoot Virgie to get at Nanz. He wanted Virgie dead, anyway.

Brent left his hiding place and ran after the two of them going up the east side of the creek. He wondered where the Kurtzmans were. And where was Dix? And Zarada? It seemed as though the canyon held only Nanz and Virgie and himself.

Brent was getting tired by the time he had

followed Nanz the length of the canyon. Even as strong as Nanz was, he must be about worn out dragging Virgie all this way. He doubted if she was making things any easier for him.

Brent was still faced with the same dilemma, stopping Nanz without risking injury to Virgie. Ahead, he could see Gunsight Rock. Apparently Nanz was aiming to take Virgie out of the canyon that way. With Virgie as hostage, he might make it. He'd know that nobody but Dix would risk shooting at him while he held Virgie.

Brent was only a hundred yards behind the pair when they broke out of the trees onto the rocky slope leading up to Gunsight Rock. There were trees dotted over the slope, but not enough to hide Nanz's movements.

Brent realized that Nanz didn't want to risk firing his gun if he didn't have to. That would bring every man in the canyon to the spot. Still Brent kept out of effective range until Nanz was well up the slope.

He considered his alternatives carefully. If he let Nanz take Virgie past Gunsight Rock, he'd never see her alive again. If he crowded Nanz now, she might be killed here. But that would be no worse.

Moving out of the trees, he ran forward. Nanz saw him and wheeled, holding Virgie in front of him.

'You come any closer and she gets it,' Nanz yelled.

'You'll never get out of the canyon,' Brent shouted back.

Nanz backed up the slope, keeping his eyes on Brent. Brent followed at the same speed, looking for a safe target to shoot at. There was none.

Then Nanz, unable to see where he was backing, caught a heel on a rock and staggered. Although he caught himself quickly, just for an instant he had released his grip on Virgie. She threw herself sideways, landing in a heap and rolling down the hill.

Brent barely saw what happened to her. His eyes were on Nanz and his gun. Nanz, realizing he had lost his protection, fired at Brent even though he was staggering to catch his balance. Brent stopped dead still and took aim. The distance was too far for six-gun accuracy but he would lose any advantage he had if he tried to get closer.

He fired twice, taking time between shots to aim. Nanz fired three shots in the same space of time but none of the bullets came close to Brent. Nanz was staggered by both of Brent's bullets and he sat down awkwardly. As Brent ran forward, Nanz let his gun drop and slowly toppled forward, his head bumping his knees before he rolled sideways.

Brent wheeled toward Virgie who was just getting to her feet. He had barely reached her when he felt something burn his shoulder. The next instant, he heard the report of a rifle.

Throwing himself down behind a rock and dragging Virgie down with him, he tried to see who had fired at him.

He caught a glimpse of a big man dodging through the rocks to get closer. Dix! He had a rifle and Brent had only a revolver. Dix wanted both Virgie and Brent dead, and he wouldn't care which one he killed first.

CHAPTER SEVENTEEN

'Keep down,' Brent warned. 'He wants you dead more than he does me.'

'Is that Dix?' Virgie asked.

Brent nodded. 'Nanz must not have been working with Dix as we thought.'

'He was trying to get me out of the canyon without Dix knowing it.'

Brent's mind was probing for some plan to get out of this spot. He'd have to do something fast. Dix could maneuver out there beyond revolver range until he got one of them in his rifle sights.

'Maybe this'll bring your pa and brothers into the fracas,' Brent said.

'Not Pa,' Virgie said softly. 'He beat Tolly last night and Tolly's dog killed him.'

Brent stared at Virgie. If Joel Kurtzman was dead, then one side of the triangle was gone. Of course, there was still Zeke, but he would be aimless without Joel's guidance. Lud would never do anybody any harm if Joel wasn't there threatening and goading him.

Brent looked up at Gunsight Rock. If they could only reach that and get over into the other canyon! He knew almost immediately though that he and Virgie could never make it. Dix would pick them off with his rifle. There wasn't enough cover on the slope.

'We'll have to try for the gap,' Brent said. 'We can't go over the top.'

'We're a long way from the trees in any direction,' she said.

He nodded. She was right. But they couldn't stay here, either, and wait for Dix to pick them off. He stretched up above the rock enough to locate Dix. In another fifty yards, he'd be around where he could get a shot at one of them.

'We're going to have to do something,' Brent said as he weighed their chances of making it to a rock thirty yards away which offered better protection.

Then suddenly another rifle opened up from down in the trees. Brent ducked at first, then realized that the bullets were not coming at them. He stretched above the rock to look down into the trees. The rifleman was aiming at Dix.

Dix had wheeled around behind a rock for protection, but now his back was exposed to Brent. It was still out of revolver range, but it was worth a bullet anyway. Brent aimed at Dix and fired. The bullet dug up the dirt fifteen yards short of Dix but it made the big man scurry for another rock and crouch between it and a tree where he had some protection from both sides.

'Suppose that's Zeke?' Brent said.

'Maybe,' Virgie said. 'But the way he took on when he saw Pa dead, I didn't think he'd go hunting again unless it was to kill Tolly's dog.'

It suddenly hit Brent. Zarada! He'd almost forgotten about him in his effort to rescue Virgie from Nanz. Brent looked around. If Dix stayed where he was now, he and Virgie could slip away to those other rocks and then on to the trees. Zarada was keeping Dix pinned down.

'Come on,' Brent said, taking Virgie's hand. 'Keep low and run hard.'

He kept his gun in his other hand and started out in a crouching run. Virgie kept pace with him. No shots came their way as they ducked behind some rocks twenty yards farther away from Dix. Dix apparently had his hands full with Zarada.

After catching his breath, Brent led the way to the other rocks, and finally to the trees close to the canyon wall. Not a shot had come their way. With the trees as protection, Brent and Virgie ran down the slope to the valley floor where the aspens were thick.

They were resting almost even with the

Kurtzman house when Zarada caught up with them.

'Where's Dix?' Brent asked.

'Still back in the rocks, I hope,' Zarada said. 'I had him hunkered down like a rabbit and he hadn't showed his face for a long time. He'll follow as soon as he's sure I'm gone.'

'We'd better hurry,' Brent said

Zarada nodded. 'I'll agree to that. Where are the Kurtzmans?'

'They're out of it, I think,' Brent said. 'Joel met with an accident and is dead. I know Lud won't fight if Joel isn't there to prod him, but I don't know about Zeke.'

Zarada nodded. 'Maybe we'll make it then. You go ahead. I'll stay behind and watch for Dix. I've got the rifle.'

Brent didn't argue with him. He wanted to get Virgie safely out of the canyon as quickly as possible. They ran on. Brent was surprised at how well Virgie stood up to the pace. She didn't complain but he did stop for rest more often than he cared to.

'Any chance Zeke'll be guarding the gap?' Brent asked once as they stopped to catch their breath.

'I don't think so,' Virgie panted. 'He'll be in those rocks to the right if he is.'

Brent knew where the guard's hiding spot was. But as they approached the end of the canyon, he didn't see any stirring around the rocks. Still holding Virgie's hand, more because he liked it than because she needed the guidance, he led her through the gap, barely able to keep their feet out of the little stream of water that ran over the bare rocks.

Beyond was the big canyon. A large stream cut through the center of the canyon, running at right angles to the little stream coming from the smaller canyon. Virgie stopped and stared at the high walls and the wide floor of the big canyon, which she hadn't seen since Joel had taken her through here to Gunsight Canyon three years ago.

Virgie continued to look but Brent tugged her on. 'You'll have plenty of time to look at the canyon after we get far enough ahead of Dix to be safe,' he said.

Brent turned down the big canyon. The plains were ahead, several miles away. Out there was Bitter Creek and Pool ranch. Even farther out was Greeley where Brent had to have Virgie by the day after tomorrow for the estate settlement.

Half a mile down the big canyon, Zarada, almost exhausted, caught up with them while they were resting. Brent looked back.

'Think Dix will follow us?'

'He has to get rid of Virgie or he won't get Pool,' Zarada panted. 'He's not about to give up.'

'You should have killed him back there,' Brent said.

'Don't think I didn't try,' Zarada said. 'If I'd

200

gotten careless, though, I wouldn't be here now. Dix is handy with a rifle, too.'

Before they had covered another half mile, Brent, who was leading, suddenly threw up his hands. 'Somebody's coming on horses.'

They ducked down into some rocks near the south wall of the canyon. Brent turned to Zarada. 'How did you get up here? Didn't you ride a horse?'

Zarada nodded. 'I rode the old white pony. I tied her just a little way from the mouth of Gunsight Canyon. But she must have got loose somehow. I looked for her when I came out but she was gone. Once she's loose, she'd head right back for home.'

Brent understood that. But it meant they'd have to walk all the way out of the canyon and maybe even farther if they couldn't borrow or buy horses somewhere.

'What about Dix and Nanz? Didn't they have horses?'

'If they did, they hid them pretty well,' Zarada said. 'I looked for them as I went in. Figured on turning them loose so they couldn't trail me when I got out. They may be afoot, but we are, too.'

The sound of horses grew louder. Three riders came into sight. Brent recognized Rudy Grubb, the sheriff. He didn't immediately recognize the two men with him.

'Dix's men,' Zarada said softly as they came closer. He fingered his rifle. 'Shouldn't shoot a

201

sheriff,' he muttered. 'But if we let them get by, then Dix will have three men to help him.'

'They've all got rifles, too,' Brent said. 'You're the only one here with a rifle. If you start something, they're liable to finish it.'

With a sigh, Zarada agreed. 'Better let them past. Then we'll hustle out of here. Dix won't know where we went for sure, and we can hide easily since we don't have horses to keep out of sight.'

The three riders went on up the canyon and Brent, Frank and Virgie resumed their trek toward the plains, staying close now to the south wall. Brent had no illusions about what Grubb and the two XD men would do. They'd join forces with Dix. Up to now, he and Zarada seemed to have had a good chance against a single man like Dix. But now the odds were again heavily in favor. Four men against two, and Dix's men had horses. What had looked like a race to get out of the canyon now threatened to become a desperate battle; one that held little promise of victory for the fugitives.

As they moved down the canyon, Zarada again dropped back a quarter of a mile behind Brent and Virgie, watching for pursuit. There was no doubt in Brent's mind that it would come. But they had to have advance warning if they were to survive.

As darkness fell over the canyon, Brent began looking for a place to camp for the night. It would be too risky to try to go on down the canyon after dark. Dix and his men might try to catch up with them in the dark and if they were stumbling along in the canyon, they'd be as easy to find as a blind bear in a closet.

Brent located a ledge perhaps thirty feet above the canyon floor. There was an overhang of bluff above it that offered protection from the chilly night air. It would make a good camp but they wouldn't dare light a fire. The flickering blaze would be visible for miles from this ledge unless a crook in the canyon blocked it off.

Brent and Virgie waited until Zarada, still keeping an eye to the rear, came along. He looked over the campsite and gave his approval. Zarada was in a hurry to get out of the canyon but he agreed with Brent that it'd be foolhardy to try to go on in the dark with Dix and his men behind them.

Brent took the first watch. After making sure Virgie was comfortable in a little hollow under the overhang, he went out to the lip of the ledge and settled down where he could listen for any sound along the canyon floor.

He and Zarada had agreed on four-hour shifts. Brent's time would be up before midnight and he'd come back on duty a while before dawn. He thought that a four-hour loss of sleep would be enough for Zarada. He was not a young man anymore.

The hours crept by and Brent listened carefully. A few times he heard deer move along below him, but nothing as heavy and awkward as a horse.

Then before midnight, Zarada took his turn, Brent went back to a spot under the overhang and fell asleep immediately. He woke up well before dawn. He couldn't be sure of the time but the canyon had not yet started to lighten up.

Moving quietly out to the ledge, he found Zarada on the alert. He signaled that he would take over.

'Think maybe they went along the canyon about an hour ago,' Zarada said. 'Couldn't be sure what it was but some kind of animals went by down there.'

'I'll keep an eye open both ways,' Brent promised.

Zarada returned to the overhang and Brent set his eyes up the canyon. If Dix and his men really had slipped down the canyon, they weren't liable to come back.

Brent was surprised to hear Zarada coming back to the lookout post just as the first gray streaks of dawn began filtering into the canyon. Brent turned toward him, but didn't see the gun until Zarada was within a few feet of him.

'What's the idea of that?' Brent demanded. 'I don't hear anybody down there.'

'I don't, either. So let's keep this quiet.'

Brent frowned. 'What do you mean by that?'

'You got Virgie out of the canyon for me,' Zarada said. 'And I appreciate that. Now I don't need you anymore.'

Brent chilled at the significance of Zarada's words. 'So you're going to get rid of me and take over Pool yourself?'

'You do catch on fast,' Zarada said. 'But I'm not a killer unless I have to be.'

'Do you think Virgie will turn over Pool to you?

'Of course she will,' Zarada said. 'After all, you and I did rescue her from that canyon. I'm sure she'll be grateful. And when she hears that you've finished your job and gone back where you came from, she'll understand that, too.'

'You're going to start me out on foot now for Nebraska?' Brent said.

'Oh, no. I'm going to tie you up where you can't interfere with any of my plans. Then when I've got the estate settled at Greeley tomorrow, I'll come back and turn you loose. I'll even pay you for the work you've done on Pool.'

'You think Virgie will swallow that lie about me leaving her before we're even sure we're out of danger from Dix?'

'She'll believe it if I tell her. She has absolutely no reason to doubt me—anymore than you had.'

Brent couldn't argue with that logic. He certainly had been taken in. He considered a half-dozen things as fast as his mind could work but he discarded them quickly. He wouldn't have a chance to draw his gun and beat Zarada. Zarada would shoot if it came to that. This was the culmination of a sixteen-year dream for him. He'd wanted Pool ranch all the time and had decided on this way to get it. It had taken careful planning. He wouldn't let it slip away now for lack of pulling the trigger once.

'I found a nice little cove around the corner from our campsite,' Zarada said. 'You'll be comfortable there. And I'll be back to turn you loose right after the settlement at Greeley.'

Zarada prodded the gun into Brent's ribs and Brent moved in the direction Zarada pointed. The dawn light was seeping into the canyon now and it wouldn't be long before it would be light enough to travel. Probably as soon as Brent was tied up, Zarada would rouse Virgie and they'd be on their way out of the canyon.

Zarada was handy with ropes, which he had in his pockets, apparently for this very task. When Brent was seated in the little hollow, back under the overhang around the corner from the camp, Zarada tied him securely and then put a gag in his mouth.

'Don't like to do that,' he said. 'But I can't have you yelling your head off and letting

Virgie know what's going on. Just take it easy and you'll be all right till I get back.'

Zarada left Brent and went back to the edge of the shelf and squatted down. By tipping his head as far forward as possible, Brent could just barely see Zarada on the ledge.

Brent tested every knot and found them all tight. He wasn't going to get out of these ropes without help. Funny thing, he thought, he was worrying more about what Virgie would think of him when Zarada told her he had run out than he was about having to sit here for two days or more bound up like a calf at the branding fire. He'd lose his lease on the Pool ranch, too; something Zarada had promised Brent if he got Virgie out of Gunsight Canyon. Suddenly he saw Zarada stand up to look out over the canyon. It was light enough now to see pretty well. Evidently Zarada thought it was time to be moving out.

Brent saw Zarada stagger just before he heard the report of the rifle. He lunged against his ropes. From the way Zarada fell, he was sure he had been hit hard. It must have been Dix who had fired the shot. Now Dix would come up here looking for Virgie. He'd find her and kill her, and Brent wouldn't be able to do a thing about it.

CHAPTER EIGHTEEN

Struggling as he was against the ropes that held him, Brent didn't see Virgie when she first came running up to where Zarada had fallen. The rifle roared again and rocks splintered from the cliff behind Virgie. She instinctively dropped down flat on the ledge.

Brent lunged against the ropes again, lost his balance and rolled out of the little cove where Zarada had put him. The commotion he made caught Virgie's attention.

Without getting up, she crawled toward him. Once back from the lip of the shelf, she got to her hands and knees. Then she was running in a crouch toward him.

'What happened?' she demanded. Then she saw the gag in his mouth and jerked it loose. 'Who did this?'

'Zarada,' Brent said. 'Can you get my hands free? Dix will be here in a minute and I need Zarada's rifle.'

Her fingers flew as she worked on the ropes. It seemed to Brent that she struggled an eternity with the knots. He could hear someone down below the ledge lumbering through the brush and over the rocks. They'd both be shot down like coyotes if Virgie couldn't get those ropes off quickly.

Then the ropes fell from his wrists and they

both tackled the ones on his ankles. Those came loose quicker and he got to his feet, running in a crouch toward the rim of the ledge where Zarada still lay. Brent dropped on his hands and knees before he reached Zarada. Grabbing the rifle, he levered a shell into it then lifted his head slowly.

The rifleman fired before Brent saw where he was. But the bullet snapped past his head and chipped more rock off the cliff behind.

Brent dropped on his belly and slid forward. He knew now approximately where the rifleman was. At the edge of the shelf, he pushed the rifle barrel over, then lifted his head to see. The man down there was circling to get a better shot. Brent had a hard time getting a sight on him and suddenly the man wheeled and fired at the ledge. Brent answered the fire before he ducked out of sight.

When he looked again, the man was farther down the slope, running hard. He fired three shots at him, not sure that any of them found their target. But it lent great speed to the disappearing gunman. He evidently hadn't expected to find anyone up here on the ledge who could fire a rifle after he downed the man standing guard.

Virgie crawled up close to Brent. 'Is he gone?'

'Like a scared rabbit,' Brent said. 'Looks like more of them down there a ways.' He pointed.

'We'll have to get out of here before they all come after us.'

Brent nodded and turned to Zarada. He wasn't dead, as Brent thought. But the bloody spot on the front of his jacket told Brent he wasn't liable to live long. A fleck of bloody froth was on his lips.

'Got to tell you something,' he said, his voice little more than a whisper.

Brent and Virgie moved closer. 'We're listening,' Brent said.

'Sorry about tying you up,' Zarada said. 'Wanted Pool for myself. There's—there's a box in my house under my bed.' He stopped and coughed and more blood showed on his lips. 'There's a paper in the box for you, Brent.'

'Why me?' Brent asked.

'Get it—you'll see. I put it there—just in case I didn't get back and you did.'

Zarada seemed satisfied now that he had gotten his message across to Brent. He heaved a big sigh and seemed to settle down into the rock itself. A minute later, his breathing stopped.

'What did he mean about wanting Pool for himself?' Virgie asked.

'Zarada has been administrator of your father's estate and he figured you'd deed Pool ranch over to him for taking care of it all these years. He had promised me that I could have a long lease on it if I would bring you out of Gunsight Canyon in time for the settlement. I guess he figured I wouldn't give up my lease so he was planning to make me disappear until he got the ranch himself.'

Virgie looked at Zarada. 'I wouldn't have thought that of him.'

'I didn't, either,' Brent admitted. 'We'd better get going. Look down there.'

Brent counted four horses moving along the floor of the canyon. Dix had evidently had his horse safely hidden where Zarada couldn't find it.

'How can we get away from them when they've got horses?' Virgie asked.

'We've got to try,' Brent said. 'There's nothing else for us to do.'

Leading the way, he left the ledge and ducked into the trees that grew along the slope of the canyon walls. It wasn't likely that Dix could get his horses up here.

Brent kept a close watch on the canyon for the riders. He realized that all they had to do was wait until Brent and Virgie reached the end of the canyon. Then they would be out in the open if they tried to cross the plains to get to Greeley. And if they didn't get to Greeley by tomorrow, Dix would get Pool without a struggle. The odds were still all against Virgie receiving her rightful inheritance.

Brent stopped occasionally to look for the riders and saw them forge ahead. He didn't know whether or not they knew where he and Virgie were. If they did, they must be planning to ambush them somewhere.

A half hour later, Brent and Virgie came to another side canyon. They'd have to come down off the slope to cross that canyon mouth in order to continue down the big canyon. Dix would know that and set his trap there, if an ambush was his plan.

Brent stopped on the slope above the canyon mouth and studied the area carefully. He soon spotted two horses tied in some trees not far from the canyon mouth. Carefully scanning the area around the horses, he finally located the riders. They were in the trees directly below Brent, a hundred yards from the horses. If he and Virgie had gone straight ahead, they'd have walked right into the waiting arms of the two men.

Brent showed Virgie the two horses and the two waiting men directly below. He continued to search the area until he saw the other horses up the side canyon. Their riders were with them. Even at this distance, Brent was sure he recognized Dix as one of the men. Dix apparently thought that Brent and Virgie might try to slip into the side canyon and escape that way.

'They figure on catching us as we cross the mouth of that side canyon,' Brent said softly.

'How can we get past them?' Virgie asked worriedly.

'We're not going down where they expect us to. We'll go down to our left into the big canyon. Maybe we can slip up to those two horses down there. If we can, then we'll have horses and two of them won't.'

A light sparkled in Virgie's eyes. 'We'll fool the foolers.'

Brent nodded and started quietly down the slope to the big canyon floor. In no time, they had dropped out of sight of the men waiting in ambush at the mouth of the side canyon. Brent was placing his hopes on the fact that the four men had not spotted them and would wait patiently for another half hour.

In the trees that fringed the canyon floor, Brent turned down the big canyon again. When he got near the little grove where he'd seen the horses, he paused to make sure they were still there and still unattended. So far as he could see, everything was just as it had been.

Cautioning Virgie to move quietly and keep up with him, he led the way through the trees toward the horses. Only for the last few feet to the horses would they be exposed to the sight of the men lying in ambush and then only if one of them happened to look their way. Brent led Virgie as close as they could go without being seen then halted.

'When we go, we'll run,' he said softly. 'If the horses are wild, we're going to be in trouble. If the men see us, you untie the horses while I keep them busy with my rifle.'

Virgie nodded. If she was scared, she hid it well. Brent checked the rifle. He had a shell jacked into the barrel so all he had to do was cock the hammer and pull the trigger.

'Now!' he whispered.

They dashed across the open space and reached the trees where the horses were tied. The horses reared back but made little noise doing it. Virgie untied one and Brent flipped the reins loose on the other. But before he could mount, a man over in the side canyon yelled. Handing the reins to Virgie, Brent wheeled. The man was swinging his rifle toward them and Brent fired. The man flinched and dived behind some trees.

Brent boosted Virgie onto one horse, then fired another shot at the other XD man before mounting himself. Once out of the trees, it was going to be a horse race. Dix and the mounted men with him were sure to give chase.

The horses hadn't been run today. They hadn't had to hurry to get ahead of Brent and Virgie on foot. Now they were ready to run and Brent set a breakneck pace. Virgie hadn't ridden much in the three years she had been in Gunsight Canyon, but she proved she was no stranger to the saddle.

Brent kept an eye on the back trail. He saw Dix and his man come charging out of the side canyon but they were far behind. After the horses had worn the edge off their enthusiasm,

Brent reined them down.

They reached the end of the canyon and Brent set a course directly for Frank Zarada's place. He needed to know what Zarada had in that box for him. From Zarada's they'd go to Greeley and be there for tomorrow's estate settlement.

At Zarada's, Brent dismounted, confident they had left Dix far behind. Hurrying inside, Brent went directly to the bed and looked underneath it.

'That must be it,' Virgie said excitedly as Brent pulled out a box.

Brent nodded and opened the box. A paper was lying right on top and he guessed this was the one Zarada had wanted him to find. He took it out of the box and read it to Virgie.

'I killed Mike Foley, Dix's man. He was snooping around too much. Any judge will know I wouldn't lie about this.' It was signed by Frank Zarada.

'Were you accused of killing him?' Virgie asked.

Brent nodded. 'That old codger knew I'd be accused of it,' he said. 'He had it planned that way just to make sure I'd go up there to get you out.'

'Are you sorry?'

Brent looked up quickly at the tone of her voice. She was looking at him with an expression he hadn't seen on her face before. The paper in his hand that was so important to him was suddenly forgotten.

'No matter what happens, I'll never be sorry about that,' he said softly.

As if to challenge his statement, a clatter of hoofbeats rattled in the yard. Brent dodged to the window. Dix was out there with two other men. He must have found another XD rider.

'You can come out any time, Brent,' Dix shouted. 'Or you can stay right in there and rot.'

Brent realized the spot he was in. He'd have to fight his way out again. Dix had already sent his men toward the barn and a shed. As long as Brent and Virgie stayed inside the house, they would be comparatively safe. But so would Dix. Tomorrow Dix would inherit Pool ranch if Virgie didn't show up to claim it.

'Let him have the ranch,' Virgie said. 'I don't want you to risk your life any more just for that.'

'Knowing Dix, I'd say we're fighting for more than just the ranch. He'll never feel safe as long as either one of us is alive.'

'We can fight them off from here, can't we?' she said hopefully.

Brent glanced out at the gathering dusk. Clouds were obscuring the sky. He saw two more riders coming and recognized one as Rudy Grubb, the sheriff. He wondered where they had gotten the horses.

Dix had disappeared behind the barn and a few rifle shots were fired, none of them dangerously close to those in the house. Just a reminder to stay out of sight, Brent knew. Dix had something else in mind. He didn't dare let Brent and Virgie live.

Darkness settled down and Brent motioned Virgie over to the window. 'Can you shoot a gun toward the barn once in a while?'

'I won't hit anything just shooting at the barn,' Virgie said.

He nodded in satisfaction. She wasn't afraid. 'I just want them to think I'm doing it. Keep out of sight yourself.'

'Where are you going?'

'Out,' Brent said. 'I'm depending on you.'

He slipped into the bedroom and across to the window through which he had left this house only a week ago. It seemed more like a year. Dix might have a man watching the back. If so, he'd have to slip past him.

Inching over the window sill, he dropped to the ground and crouched there, listening. Hearing nothing, he moved silently around the corner of the house then out away from it. Close to the barn, he stopped. There were three men at the corner of the barn. He couldn't hear what they were saying but it was obvious they were planning something.

Then the three disappeared in the darkness, going different directions. When Brent saw Dix next, a fire was outlining his huge frame up by the house, and he realized that Dix had set fire to the house. He planned to kill them as they tried to escape the flames. Brent was safe from the fire but Virgie was still in there. Brent had to get her out.

'You can come out or you can burn,' Dix yelled. 'Makes no difference to me.'

Brent saw that Dix had placed himself safely between two windows where anyone inside could not get a shot at him. But he hadn't planned on Brent being out here.

'I'll be right out,' Brent shouted from the darkness.

Dix whirled, his gun in his hand. But the fire was the only light and it was behind him.

'Over here,' Brent shouted.

Dix fired at the sound and Brent fired twice, having a perfect target outlined against the fire.

Dix toppled forward. Still Brent didn't dare show himself. He couldn't wait, either, or he might not be able to get Virgie out of the burning house.

'Grubb,' he yelled. 'Dix is dead. You want to die, too?'

'I've had enough,' one man yelled. 'I can't stomach burning a woman out of a house.'

'We're leaving,' another voice shouted. Brent recognized that as Grubb's voice.

He didn't wait to see if they meant it. He dashed for the house. No bullets sought him out. He hit the door and crashed through. Virgie was still next to the window, holding the rifle.

Grabbing her by the hand, he pulled her out the door, close to the flames which were reaching up the side of the house. They couldn't save the house but Brent still had the paper that Zarada had signed.

Outside they stopped and watched the house burn. Dix's men were all gone. Only Dix lay close to the house.

'We have to be in Greeley tomorrow,' Brent said. 'Let's start now. If you don't get there, you won't own that ranch.'

'I won't keep it,' Virgie said.

Brent stared at her in surprise. 'What are you going to do with it?'

'Sell it to the man who's leasing it,' she said. 'I don't want the ranch. But I do want the man who will own it.' She looked at him with an innocence that belied her words. 'Do I get him?'

'You've got him,' Brent said, and meant every word of it.